SPELLBOUND

Pete Fanning

IMMORTAL WORKS
SALT LAKE CITY

Immortal Works LLC
1505 Glenrose Drive
Salt Lake City, Utah 84104
Tel: (385) 202-0116

© 2022 Pete Fanning
www.petefanning.com

Cover Art by Lenore Stutznegger
www.lenorestutz.com

ISBN 978-1-953491-43-5 (Paperback)
ASIN B0BD5ZWFK2 (Kindle)

To Liz, the best little sister a guy could ask for.

Chapter 1

I t's mayhem outside of Peakland Middle School. Stampedes bust through the exits, and kids scatter in all directions. Some flee toward the parking lot, others seek the safety of the football field or farther still, the abandoned railroad tracks in the nearby woods. One boy has climbed the flagpole.

A mass evacuation is in order. This is not a test.

The schoolyard is a battlefield of debris. Notebook paper, textbooks, book bags, discarded masks, hall passes, gym towels, an abandoned tennis shoe—at least one tuba—litter the grounds. Those who haven't fled huddle in chattering groups near the pick-up lane, eyes are wide and abuzz after the early dismissal was issued.

A line of honking minivans and SUVs snake around the school parking lot, slowing only enough to allow kids to hop in before they go screeching out of the lot before the door can even be shut.

I can't help the swell of pride that finds my chest, although this is no time to enjoy my handiwork. My two best friends, okay, *only* friends, Chuck Tinsley and Ahmad Das stand loyally by my side, taking in the scene on this otherwise sunny and warm fall day. I wipe my hair back, wondering whether I've gone too far or haven't done enough.

The moment is short-lived, zapped like a pulled plug when my brother comes charging through the crowd, making his way toward me. I take a breath and hold my eye roll. Colton's not in a rush because he's worried about my safety, that I can assure you. He's on to me, but I expected as much, even from him.

Sure enough, here he comes, to chide me like a disobedient dog. "Abby." His face is flushed, his eyes scan the grounds. "Abby. You need to fix this, fast."

"Oh Colton, I'm so glad you're safe." I launch into him with a hug, figuring I might as well sell it.

He shoves me off. I smile for Chucky and Ahmad's benefit —they're looking a bit skittish—when Colton spins me around by the shoulder and lowers his voice. "Abby, you promised."

First of all, I did no such thing and he knows it. Still, I set a hand to my chest, ducking away from him because his breath smells like pork rinds. "Whatever do you mean?"

Behind me, Chuck giggles. Neither he nor Ahmad have any idea what's happening, but I have their support. Blind loyalty such as theirs is hard to find these days. If you can find yourself a couple of quiet friends, ones who will stand at your side through the best and the worst, keep them close. It's probably their biggest asset.

Colton shoots Chucky a stern look that shuts him down. "This isn't funny, Chuck."

Greenie, the hall monitor/parking lot attendant, comes shoving through the crowd. He's Code Red frantic today, his stringy hair out of place, his eyes loose in their sockets as he wields a forehead thermometer like a gun. The early dismissal clearly has him unnerved—which isn't saying a lot as far as Greenie is concerned. Under normal circumstances Greenie is only a hall pass away from a breakdown. Now, with a couple hundred kids gathered on the curb, the lawn, the sidewalks, left to mill about without order—well, he's never going to make it.

He fights through the madness, shaking the beeping thermometer, shooing people into place, shouting orders:

"Single file!"

"Away from the curb."

"All right, all right, no pushing or shoving."

"No yelling."

"You! Come here, now!"

"Hey, who spit chewing gum on the sidewalk?"

Poor Greenie. It's his worst nightmare come to fruition. And I know all too well about living-nightmares. It happened to me a mere two months ago, when I left out an "R" in "embarrass" during the final round of the national spelling bee. Talk about irony.

Greenie's voice cracks, and the sweat patch on his back looks like a world map. I watch him scurry about, bending over to examine a sock, when Colton waves for my attention.

He lowers his voice. "Abby, it's just that..." He looks around, checking to make sure no one is paying attention. They're not, how could they? Not with the ambulance hitting the siren twice as it pulls out onto the street. "We said no more spells."

No more spells. *Oh* the nerve. The spell thing only began last year after he was cast as a fairy for a school play. I was messing around with his props—wand, wings, glitter—and stumbled across something that worked. Next thing I knew, he was doing all sorts of crazy things on the football field—running, jumping, zipping around. He set high school football records even though he was only in the seventh grade. And now, because things didn't end so well for him, he's going to tell me right from wrong? Please.

"Abby."

"What?"

"No more spells," he repeats, looming over me, waiting for me to buckle.

Ridiculous. Here I have the power to stop evil. I can right wrongs, small and large. I've discovered a way to single-handedly balance the power between the strong and the weak. And I'm supposed to stand to the side and watch, turn the other cheek, betray those in need? No thanks.

I shrug and pat him on the shoulder. "Relax, bro."

He looks at my hand, then me. "Bro?"

I roll my eyes. Sometimes, with Colton, you have to s-p-e-l-l things out. Or you fix things, sit back, and let him think he's making the call. "It should wear off by nightfall."

His eyes bug out. "So it *was* you?"

"Duh." I sigh, looking around. A faint *thump thump thumping* overhead.

"And what do you mean, *should* wear off? Please tell me Chaz Snead will be okay."

"Fine. It *will* wear off. Stupid Chaz will be completely fine. And hopefully he will have learned a very valuable lesson."

The news station chopper makes a fly over. Hmm, I have to admit, I wasn't planning on this much media attention. However, Mr. Wolff, our new principal, doesn't seem rattled in the least. In fact, he's especially calm, walking among us with his hands clasped behind his back as he checks on students, parents, and staff with a creepy big smile on his odd face.

A crash out in the street steals my attention from Mr. Wolff. A minivan has rear-ended an SUV. Traffic on Eastwood grinds to a halt. Police cars, sirens, the news—it's all a bit much. But sometimes that's what it takes for a bully to learn a valuable life lesson.

Yes, I did it. Because Target #1, Chaz Snead, has terrorized Peakland Middle school without consequence for far too long. He goes after the short, the weak, the quiet, the, *ahem*, moderately average. Google "Bully" and Chaz Snead appears amidst a string of algorithms and keywords. Just last week he dumped cayenne pepper in Morty Grabowski's gym shorts. But long before that, I'd decided Chaz Snead was no good, and he deserved what he got. The algorithm has changed.

Hmm, I like the sound of that.

Honestly though, I might have left him off my list had he not started in with Chuck. I have a weakness for underdogs. And Chuck, with his corduroy pants and off-brand tennis shoes, is like a runt under a porch. So the other day when Chaz called Chuck "Splotch," then "Smear," referring to the birthmark on my friend's cheek (I think it's shaped like Italy), it got my attention. And when Chuck's lip started quivering like he was going to start crying in class, well, Chaz Snead found himself at the top of my newly formed hit-list.

That was the day he became Target #1.

And now, having put Chaz in his place, Colton is telling me to knock it off? The nerve. Funny how things change. Again, the nerve, I tell you.

Looking out to the street, I watch parents argue over right-of-way and signals. It's remarkable how frightened everyone looks, almost comical, how easy it is to shake up routine and ruin these fragile mental states. But they shouldn't be scared, so long as they behave like decent human beings.

But where there is a Target #1, there is a Target #2, and a #3.

Oh, these mortals. Don't they realize what I can do? No, they don't. And that's why it's so hard to keep the smile from splitting my face.

A few hours ago this was a mundane school day. I was eating with Chuck and Ahmad. It was a rare occasion, my two closest friends hardly ever eat lunch anymore because Chaz always does *something* obnoxious to *someone* in the cafeteria where he has an audience. I assured them both all was fine, everything was taken care of, when sure enough, Chaz strolled by and said, "Hey Smear," to Chucky, all the while oblivious to the green spots on his own face. Not to pat my own back, but it was excellent work. Like someone had taken a highlighter and gone to town.

Someone laughed. I pretended to read my book when another person noticed. It wasn't long before people were covering their mouths and snickering, and I was trying so hard not to lose control or give myself away. But it was a bit too excellent.

By the time Chaz took a seat with his cronies, the dots on his face had grown, multiplied, and ripened to a bright, radioactive sheen. I could only stare, in awe of what I'd done. Me and everyone else.

Chairs scraped the floor. Soon Chaz found himself alone at the table, looking at his arms as a buzz came over the cafeteria.

Chaz's sunken eyes emerged from their pits as nuclear splotches formed on his skin. First dots, then spots, until he was covered completely. He pulsed to life, neon and glowing. By then it was bedlam, kids stood on chairs to get a better view. People snapped pictures and videos. Only, the laughter quickly turned to fear. Someone pulled the fire alarm. Greenie, the hall monitor, came rushing to see what was going on, skidding to a halt when he saw poor old radioactive Chaz.

Perhaps I'd overdone it. I kept my head down when the EMTs arrived, my face buried in a book as Chaz was laid out on a gurney, crying like a baby, his spikey hair matted down on one side as he called for his mommy. By then, no one was laughing. I slunk low in my chair.

When Mr. Wolff arrived, the school was cleared out. The rumors started about a biological attack. Covid-22. A new pandemic was underway.

Oops.

Now, out in the yard, it's a bit concerning how quickly my

brother has put things together. Still, there isn't much he can do about it. Is there?

My smile fades. It seems like Colton is contemplating the unthinkable. Someone bumps into me from behind, but I manage to keep my eyes locked on my brother. "Wait. You're not...you're not going to tell Mom and Dad, are you?"

He rolls his neck like he does when he's nervous. As the minivan mishap clears out and the procession gets going again, Greenie barks at the stragglers to form a line. My stomach rolls at the thought of my brother actually considering ratting me out.

But how could Colton rat me out? He, of all people, should know what it would sound like, running to the parentals and telling them his little sister is casting spells on bullies. Still, this change in the tide makes me squirm.

"Oh man, this is what I was worried about." He nods toward the parking lot, and I follow his gaze, where I find the reason for his nerves. Jada Johnson, my old journalism mentor, now a freshman reporter, is storming across the lot, headed our way.

Yikes. In the distance, the doors to Peakland High School swing open and kids come waltzing out, joking and blinking at the bright sunshine. Oh boy. It appears the entire Peakland school system is getting an early dismissal thanks to yours truly.

"Colton. Abby."

Jada waves us down, her phone in her hand, poised and ready to capture incriminating evidence. Colton scans the lot as though looking for an escape route. "Great, just what we need." He looks at me. "This needs to go away. Tonight."

I nod. Sure, I hold all the smarts in the family, but some situations call for brawn. Or in Colton's case, scrawn.

"It will," I assure him.

Jada's closing in. She's about to start with the rapid fire questions. *Hit 'em fast and hit 'em hard. And never let up,* she used to say last year when she was an eighth grader and took me under her wing.

Thankfully Dad pulls up in the van. "Hey kids, um, everything all right?"

I smile at his timing. Jada stops in her tracks, leveling a gaze at us. She cocks her head as though to say *This isn't over*.

That was close.

Chapter 2

Being let out of school early throws the day for a loop. By the time we sit for dinner, it's got more of a Saturday feel to it. Dad scoots up to his place at the table and tucks his napkin in his collar like a bib. I smile because he's got a nice sized coffee stain down the front of his shirt. Some things never change.

"So kids, what in the world, huh?"

Colton's eyes never leave me as Mom sits and folds her napkin in her lap. "Yes, oh dear, the news said it's some kind of bug? It must be serious for them to let out the entire school system."

As the two people in this family who can walk more than ten feet without tripping, my mother and I share a special bond, one I hope can withstand the pushback when or if my brother rats me out.

"Ooh. A bug. Hear that, Abby? Sounds *super* serious. I really hope it's not contagious," Colton teases.

Mom raises an eyebrow at him. I stare at my empty plate. Okay, I will admit it. I hadn't expected things to blow up the way they did. The plan was for Chaz Snead to learn a lesson, maybe take a trip to the nurse's office, get sent home, and come back reformed. Worst case scenario, Peakland Middle got out early and everything goes back to normal the next day.

"I think it's fine," I mumble. Colton scoffs, still trying to play it cool, which for him is an impossible task. He scoops out some spaghetti but drops a meatball in his lap and it rolls to the floor. Under the table, Max leaps into action. Then Dad drops his meatball and Max shimmies over to his feet. Our lively husky lives for meatball night.

Like my dad, Colton has an uncanny knack for clumsy. He can break *anything* at any time, and until I helped him out last year he was doomed, only known for his EPIC FAIRY FAIL video after he tumbled off the stage at rehearsal.

Sure, Colton's lovable, in that aww shucks kind of way, but he's not exactly going to win any academic awards—something I know all about. Not to brag, but since skipping the fifth grade and flying through the sixth, I've entered the seventh grade at eleven years old. And let me say, I'm not impressed.

Maybe that's why my family is so frustrating. Here I've never gotten anything but A's in my life, my test scores are in the top percentile *nationwide*, I write for the school paper, I'm fluent in Spanish and French, I'm on the chess team, and we've covered the casting spells thing. And yet, my parents dote on Colton like he's the last kitten in a soggy cardboard box.

It's been this way as long as I remember. *Whoopsie, Colton wrecked his bike into the only tree for miles and miles. Oops, Colton sprained his ankle in his sleep again.* Colton this and Colton that. Who knows, maybe he *is* the genius in this family, because there's something to be said about low expectations.

Mom takes a piece of garlic bread and tries to stay on track. "So, is it like a measles thing? Chicken Pox? The news was scarce on the details."

Colton's ears move with his smile. I have never once been in trouble, real trouble, and I don't plan on starting today. I widen my eyes, raise and drop my shoulders. "Yeah, I don't exactly know. One minute we were eating lunch and the next, we're told to leave. It was kind of scary, really."

Colton snorts and Dad turns to him. "Colton, this is no laughing matter. I'm glad you guys are up to date on your vaccinations. This *is* scary."

Colton glares at me. "You're right, Dad. It's not a laughing matter. I'm just glad you're okay, Abby. Really, this must be hard for you."

"Cut it out," Mom chides. Then she smiles. "Oh, Abby. Jada called for you. That nice reporter girl?"

My brother and I exchange glances. I nod. "Oh, she's probably after the scoop."

Mom smiles. "Well, today would be a big story, right? I mean, we've heard all sorts of things. Is Chaz Snead okay?"

Colton sets his glass of milk down. "Yeah, Abby, is Chaz Snead okay? You were there, right?"

My brother is only a few seconds away from growing an extra ear when Dad reels us in with super boring work talk. From there dinner discussion turns delightfully boring.

After dinner, I take off for my room so I can be alone and sort things out. I log onto my spelling bee account so I can take a practice quiz. Acing them always makes me feel better.

Thinking back to summer makes my shoulders slump. The Big Time, the National Spelling Bee. Mom and Dad, sitting in the audience as I stood next to Tanvir Antar, the other finalist. I remember my mind roaming. The lights were bright and the camera was on and I knew it was the big time, five hundred kids whittled down to two. Only him and me now. And if these kids knew what I could really do, like, put a spell on glitter to make my brother run like an Olympian sprinter, boy, wouldn't that be something.

The next thing I knew, I'd muffed an easy word.

Well, not this year. I log in and start banging out words.

Gossiping

Guarantee

Grievance

How could I lose? I know these words backward. I'm in a good groove, and it feels good to let the stress of the day roll off my back as the letters float and sort themselves in my head. It's always been this way, ever since I can remember. I *see* the letters vividly, like I can reach out and grab them. At least until Colton tries to barge in but runs into the door with a *thunk*.

I shake my head, laughing. Because it's too easy. What a doofus.

He bangs on the door three times. "Abby, let me in."

I find my notebook and shove it under the pillow. When I open the door he barges in. "Okay, so un-spell him."

"What?"

He plops down on my bed and eyes the laptop with all the words. He fails to conceal the small smirk on his lips. "I should have known."

"What does that mean?" I think my brother secretly loves when I fail. I must say, it doesn't happen often.

"Huh? Nothing. I just, didn't know you were doing the spelling thing again."

I cross my arms. "Well, I am."

"Okay, okay." He eyes the door then lowers his voice. "So Chaz."

"So Chaz, what?"

"Un-spell him. Now."

I shoot my brother a look. "I'm sorry, when did you become my boss again?"

"Around the same time I decided not to tell Mom and Dad what you're up to, that's when."

He must really be proud of himself. To come strolling, or, banging into my room and barking orders. The clock shows 7:05. "Well, he's got another hour or so yet."

Colton leaps to his feet. "Abby, what if he's in the hospital right now? What if they're running tests on him or treating him? Think about his parents. How scared they must feel."

"Oh, Colton." I sit up, looking him over. Yep, he's actually serious. Time to take him down a peg. "Let me ask you this: when did you become so high and mighty? Last year you were practically begging me to help you. Now you storm in and demand I stop. What gives?"

"That's exactly why. Remember last year, all the trouble we caused? We messed up... I messed up. I learned my lesson. I thought we had an agreement. And besides, Jada is onto us now. Un-spell him."

I walk to the window, looking out to the yard where Mom and Dad study a dirt patch out in the garden. "You're so demanding, Colton, sheesh. You know, I'm actually doing the school a service. Heck, I'm doing the world a favor. Guys like Chaz Snead grow up and become powerful and corrupt men. They are the reason for most of our problems today. So, this," I look back at him. "This spell, should be something he remembers for the rest of his life. And hopefully, the next time—"

"Spare me the lecture, sis."

I shoot him my best glare, which isn't much. It is beyond frustrating how no one takes me seriously. Out in the yard, Dad stumbles over some weeds, but Mom helps him stay upright. They're completely clueless. I look at Colton. "Fine. I guess the lesson has been learned, anyway."

On my windowsill, I arrange my quartz stones, light the sandalwood incense, and then, although I really didn't want to do this while Colton was around, retrieve the water bottle filled with green sludge from my closet.

With my long tweezers I remove the picture of Chaz Snead

—the one I lifted off his idiotic Facebook account—from the slime and hold it over the wastebasket.

Colton's eyes go wide. "What in the world?"

I shrug. "I can't tell you all my secrets, bro."

This whole thing with Chaz isn't all that much a witchy "spell" but more biology, chemistry, perhaps a smidge of telekinesis, for lack of a better term. Something I can't quite explain. Anyway, I shake the sludge from Chaz's picture. "There, he's healing as we speak."

Colton stands and gapes, dumbfounded. Or, in his case, normally. He actually sniffs the photo like a dog, then wrinkles his nose. "Uhh, seriously, what did you do to him?"

I wipe the rest of the sludge from Chaz's stupid picture. "It's microalgae. I grew it in the closet, it only took—"

He's already backing out of my room, holding his nose and waving me off with his free hand. "You know what? I don't need to know this. So, we're good?"

I pinch my own nose to mimic his nasally voice. "Yes, Colton. We're good. So long as you don't rat me out." Then, I shoot him a smirk. "I have plenty of pictures of *you* around here."

He's out the door when he shivers, turns, looks down the hallway, and leans in. "Abby. You wouldn't."

No, I wouldn't. But it's so fun to mess with him. And yet, he's not done. "And you can't go around making people sick."

More with the dramatics. "Oh, please. I told you. he's not sick. And besides, I'm doing the public a service. I'm stopping evil."

He shakes his head. "Chaz Snead isn't evil. He's a jerk. But not *evil*."

"Not yet he isn't," I say, and then, before I can stop myself, "And he's not the only one."

He shoots me a look. "Abby, what are you planning?"

I arrange the crystals, shrug. "This is only phase one. The moon has eight phases. It's safe to say, this is the new moon."

Colton waves me off. "Um, yeah, just don't do it again."

With that, he's gone. And I get back to my words.

Chapter 3

The school admins are quick to declare our learning institutions safe, although they stress any kid too "traumatized" by the "events that took place yesterday" are welcome to stay home.

Of course, our parents send us packing. Probably because Colton is itching to get to school so he can see his girlfriend, Lani. He's still playing the role of Mr. Responsible, and it's starting to get old. He doesn't say a word to me on the walk to school, doesn't blink when I make a funny joke about food poisoning in the cafeteria. And as soon as we're safely on school grounds, he ditches me, dashing off as we're herded into the gymnasium for a school-wide "discussion" about yesterday's "events."

At least Chucky and Ahmad were thoughtful enough to save a spot for me in the second row of the bleachers. It looks as though half the school has taken the free pass on the "trauma."

"Hey guys, what's up?"

Ahmad and Chucky exchange glances. Ahmad turns to me. "Chucky heard that Chaz Snead had to be airlifted to McCliff Hospital."

"Um, what?" I turn to Chucky. "That's ridiculous. Where did you hear that?"

Chucky studies his feet. He's got chocolate in the corners of his mouth. Usually I'd hand him a tissue, but I need to know what's going on. His hands flop like fish in his lap. "My parents are friends with his neighbors. Said they wanted a series of tests performed. Yikes, huh?"

I'm ninety-seven percent sure the spell has worn off. Still, *airlifted*? Yikes. I think of all the wasted resources and staff. My chest tightens. A cool sweat finds my back. Maybe I really have made a mess out of things. But I can't let it knock me off course. Lesson learned. I shake off the worry, digging in my book bag for a Kleenex. It helps keep my hands busy. "Well, I think he's fine. I think everyone is overreacting, is all."

"I hope so."

It's endearing, Chucky's concern for a bully who has spent the past few weeks tormenting him. It warms my heart. But I need him to worry less, it's sort of messing with me and I have to stay focused.

When I first arrived at Peakland Middle, I was either teased for being so young or treated like a baby. The eighth graders liked to call me "cute" or "adorable," while some of the not so nice students asked me if I still rode in a car seat (it was a booster seat, thank you). So I have all the respect in the world for someone like Chucky, who is always so willing to forgive. It's easier said than done.

My heartwarming moment is short-lived, though, as kids jostle and shuffle past us, stepping on my bags as the buzz of rumors continue to swirl through the gym.

I spot Colton across the court, slapping hands and nodding his head like a goofball. Because of my spells, Colton is the proud owner of half a dozen *high school* football records. That's right, last year he went from third string middle school benchwarmer, to running wild on the football field. Things were great, at least until *he* took it too far. And that's why it gets to me so much, him telling *me* what *I* should do with *my* spells.

Chucky gets himself cleaned up, then he's rubbing his

palms on his lap. "I almost didn't come today. My dad thinks this could be a biological attack and..."

I restrain my eye roll. Chucky's dad writes comic books and overall is a fun guy. That said, this is a bit much.

"...it could be the beginning of a new global initiative on the..."

"Ridiculous." I cut him off much too sharply. "I mean, I think we'll be fine," I say with a pat on his arm.

Mr. Wolff enters the gym stiff and serious. The murmurs quiet immediately, and you can hear the *click-clack* of his loafers on the gym floor. The microphone screeches as he takes it in his hand, bends down to say something to an assistant, then does that thoughtful grimace thing he likes to do.

Finally, he looks over the student body the way a dictator regards his countrymen.

"I know many of you have cause for concern today. Yesterday's incident gave us all quite a scare. But after consulting with doctors and medical experts, I can assure you, with one-hundred percent certainty, that Peakland Middle School, and our town in general, is safe."

There's something I don't trust about Mr. Wolff. Maybe it's his long fingernails or cold gray eyes or the creepy little white streak through his left eyebrow, but my instincts scream out. Mr. Morton, our old principal, was the kind of guy who had a basketball half-court shot challenge before pep rallies. He was always smiling, his office open to anyone, even if he was a bit, um, gullible. He too got caught up in the glittery mess Colton made out of things last year. Probably why he's not the principal now.

Now we're stuck with this stiff as he paces back and forth, *click-clack*, letting his assurances sink in. "...as a precaution, we've had the cafeteria scrubbed and..."

I fold my arms over my chest. His curt tone, the weird little accent, how he stalks around with one hand in his pocket like this is a town hall and he's trying to show the voters he can be thoughtful yet stern, all of it irks me. Blah de bloop blah blah. It's clear he's trying to play hero, the safeguard, standing tall, as though we're fighting some unseen evil and he's keeping us safe. In reality, the exact opposite is true.

I am the one who's rid this school of one of its biggest toxins, at least for the time being, and I'm not about to watch Mr. Wolff get up there and make assurances.

Ahmad turns to me. "Abby, are you okay?"

"Huh?" I realize I'm digging my nails into my arms. "Oh, yeah, sorry. It's just boring, that's all."

Ahmad smiles that shy little smile of his, and I want to tell him and Chucky it's okay, they're safe now. This isn't some global attack or another pandemic but an act of kindness. I won't let those big bad bullies lay another finger on them. Even if Mr. Wolff is up there stealing my thunder.

"It appears this was a onetime thing, a medical anomaly, if you will. But we do have grief counselors on standby, if anyone feels they need to talk about yesterday's events."

Oh for Pete's sake. Chaz Snead is lying in a bed somewhere scarfing down ice cream and bingeing Netflix. He's fine, completely fine. It's mind-numbing, only my mind doesn't numb but tingles. And before I can finish the thought, I'm training my glare on Mr. Wolff—who is, after all, Target #2.

Yes, our very own principal is a target. And what he's doing now only justifies his place on the list. Only, not now, I should wait. The plan is still in the developing stages.

"We are completely safe here. I want to reiterate..."

Seeing our new principal up there on his high horse, the clickity-clack of his hooves, reminds me of a field trip we took two years ago to a farm in the country. Everyone loved watching the horses grazing. Tall and muscular. But I was drawn to the donkey, grayish in color, with a black mane spilling over his long head. His sad eyes...

Mr. Wolff's pacing, his arrogant grandstanding, it's more than I can take. It feels like a corkscrew twisting around in my chest. Suddenly, I'm no longer in control of my senses. I'm stuck between my annoyance and the field trip memory, when Mr. Wolff kicks out suddenly and sends the microphone stand flying across the gym.

A quick gasp and the student section breaks out into laugher.

"Nothing is funny here. This is not a laughing. Ehhhhh."

A donkey's whinny escapes his mouth. Ahmad covers his smile. The laughter grows. Mr. Wolff coughs and picks up the mic stand, but when he does both legs kick out behind him and he's braying like a, you know...

Donkey.

The bleachers lose it. And I'm looking left and right, ready to slink away when Mr. Wolf's ears grow tall and furry—and then the screaming starts.

Once again, Mr. Wolff attempts to restore order, but now from the back of his pants hangs a tail like a rope, swishing around, batting away nonexistent flies. I cover my mouth with one hand but keep my gaze trained on my target. The bleacher section has gone hysterical, one-part laughter and the rest urgent screams. Mr. Wolff's hands fly to his giant ears but it's too late. It's now a circus.

I should stop. I should stop this right now.

People are standing, pointing, grinning and laughing, but the laughing is quickly turning into a sweeping panic over the student section. While our principal brays and kicks, the mic cord snakes around his ankles, he bucks his legs and chairs go flying. And then he's on all fours, romping around like something from a carnival. He's half principal, half donkey.

"Umph."

A collective gasp rolls through the gym as our principal flails about "Eh haw, eh haw."

His hair, now a dark mane, stands straight up on his head, his large teeth gnashing. I should stop this right away, but I won't, I can't, not when the mic screeches again on impact and Mrs. Tony, our assistant principal, hurries over to assist, but there's not much she can do.

My vision tunnels until I close my eyes and ball up my fists. I'm powerless, no longer in control of my actions. I force my eyes open as another assistant walks over along with some coaches, and soon there's a crowd trying to corral our bucking principal from the gym.

As the laughter subsides and the coaches stand back, it's clear people are beginning to link this bizarre event to the other bizarre event. I'm locked in, trying to make things right. I think Chucky is talking to me, but I can't remove my gaze from the disaster happening at midcourt.

Finally, I zap out of it. I unclench my fists and exhale. It's as though the tingles rush from my spine to my limbs and out my fingers. And there, on the Panther logo, with the overturned chairs and gaping staff, poor Mr. Wolff comes to, looking around as though he's lost. It doesn't help that the coaches have roped his neck with speaker cable, which they use to lead him out to the lobby.

The murmuring continues until Mrs. Tony rushes over, stops, looks around, finds the microphone, and picks it up. She takes another look at the door where Mr. Wolff untangles himself, shoving off the coaches. "Okay people. Single file. Let's get to class."

"Whoa, did you see that?"

Again, no idea how long Chucky has been talking to me, but I nod slowly as a chill rushes over my arms. Did I really do that?

I hadn't planned it. I shake it off. Chucky laughs. "That was like a magic trick. I wonder how they did that."

"Yeah."

Mrs. Tony directs the eighth graders out first then turns to our section, and I get to my feet and shuffle out in a daze. I look at my hands. I mean, it wasn't a spell. I hadn't planned it. I was mad about Mr. Wolff taking the credit and then... I need to get myself together.

I turn to my friends. My mouth is dry, breaths short as I try to scrape up the words. "Guys, I need to go. I mean, to the restroom."

Before they can ask if I'm okay I turn and rush off, bumping into bodies, fighting through the rush of talk and laughter, everyone gushing about Mr. Wolff and the weirdness going on at our school. I need a minute to work through what just happened, and I'm almost free when I run smack into the one person I cannot see right now.

Colton stands before me, his arms crossed over his chest. He looks me over like I'm a monster in that stupid video game he used to play. Lucky for me, Lani Andrews is with him so he won't call me out. At least not right now.

"Hi, Abby," Lani says in that super sweet way of hers. She looks around. "Was that bizarre or what?"

Definitely "or what". I like Lani, and Colton's super lucky that she likes him, but I can't do this right now. I wipe back my hair. A few beads of sweat rest on my forehead. Colton seems to notice.

I smile at Lani. "Oh, hi, Lani. Hi, Colton. Hey, I need to..."

I start to brush by them to make a mad dash for it when Colton blocks my way. "Whoa. Hang on."

My brother glances at Lani like he knows how crazy it would sound if he asks me if I spelled the new principal into a donkey. Instead, he leans closer, whispering, "This needs to stop."

I grit my teeth. He's trying so hard to be Dad. I put on my biggest, fakest smile. "Yes absolutely. Well, I'll see you guys later."

With that I scoot past them and scramble to the bathroom where I run cold water over my face. I have to get myself together. Drying off, I look at the girl in the mirror. Same old me, sandy blonde hair, oval face, blue eyes. But something's different.

I no longer look like Abby, Colton's smart baby sister, but Abby Clutts, conqueror of all things evil. And, shaken as I am, I like what I see. Because it's not every day you can wreck an entire school.

Unless you're me, that is.

With that, I'm all set to get to class and put this behind me. And I get about two steps before I run smack into Target #3.

In a world that places looks far and beyond anything else, Reagan Roebuck has been given an insurmountable head start. Tall but not towering, skinny but not lanky, she's blonde, blue, and dangerous. Today, like every day, she's with Jordan Swann, one of her flunkies, as they stroll into the bathroom, loud and blathering about the weirdness of the day.

"Oh my gosh, that was crazy."

"Yeah, like so weird."

When they see me they stop short, perhaps waiting for me to apologize for existing. And I'll admit, with Reagan Roebuck, it's hard not to clear the way and stand to the side, hoping she'll let it slide. Last year, Reagan called Natalie Wright Fat-alie until she left school and never returned.

Seconds ago I was unstoppable. Now, under the searing heat of her glare, as she and Jordan loom over me for a full five seconds, then five more, I feel myself deflating. I look to my feet and start for the door, ready to shy away and slink off to class.

After what feels like a galactic year, Reagan tilts her head and knocks back a silky strand of hair from her perfect face. "You're that spelling girl, right?"

A spark of hope hits my chest. Despite myself, I nod and open my mouth, but words don't make the trip. She *knows* me. Reagan Roebuck knows me. Hmm, maybe she shouldn't be a target after all. Maybe this is all one big misunderstanding. For a flash, a split second, I lose my senses. I picture myself walking in tow with the popular eighth grade girls. Me, Abby Clutts, having lunch with Double R and Jordan and...

"Wow, you really blew it didn't you."

My little fantasy bubble pops as they break into laughter and barge past me to the mirror, just as quickly dismissing me from their thoughts.

My shoulders drop. Ugh, how could I have thought that Reagan Roebuck—the girl who eyes the world as though it were placed under her chin like a meal at a restaurant—would let me into her circle? Or that I need her acceptance at all. I swallow up the shame, wanting to spit out my weakness.

Fine, I think to myself. *She will remain Target #3.*

I grit my teeth, ready to unleash something vile, when Reagan pries herself away from the mirror and back to me. "Oh, you're still here? Um, good*bye* little miss spell girl."

I open my mouth to speak, but you know what, it's funny. I start to chuckle, and then I can't stop, and I'm still giggling when they turn again and look at me like I'm a freak, which, I suppose I'm not helping my case.

I shake my head, waving them off. "Sorry, but I mean, get it? Miss Spell Girl. *Misspell?*" I snort. "Oh, that's good. Good stuff, Reagan."

They exchange looks, lips curled and eyebrows raised. I

shake my head. "Okay, well. Goodbye." I wave to them and make my way to class.

Phew. Close call. But from there, my fear melts away. Because yeah, I may be small and lug around two book bags, I may not have the confidence of Reagan Roebuck, but as the sun peaks out and the day goes from glum to bright, I'm okay with that. Let the students talk. Let them fear me. Because Colton is wrong. This does not have to stop. I am no longer Little Abby Clutts, brainiac eleven-year-old seventh grader, but instead I'm Abby Clutts, defender of the small and weak.

Reagan will soon find out the hard way that I am a force to be reckoned with.

Chapter 4

It's confusing. The gym, what I did without thinking. I have to be more careful. Everything is still fuzzy from the assembly. I hadn't meant to do whatever I'd done to Mr. Wolff. Sure, I had plans for him, he was Target #2 after all. But I need to space these things out more.

At the same time, I won't let it knock me off my quest. I've read scientific studies on the physical and psychological effects of positive thinking, so I know I have to look at the bright side of all this. With Targets #1 and 2 neutralized so quickly, I can take my time as I turn my attention to Reagan Roebuck. There, I feel better already.

I sit through Language Arts, my positive attitude taking a hit as Miss Crawford describes the many obstacles Helen Keller faced. It's sad to think how mercilessly Helen would've been teased by the likes of Reagan Roebuck. Harassed to tears, probably.

"Okay, let's find a partner for Think-Pair-Share."

A collective groan issues from the class. I glance around the room, casually, so not to look desperate. Chairs and desks scoot across the floor. I usually work alone, which is better for me because I finished the autobiography weeks ago. I only hope Miss Crawford doesn't push too hard about the partner thing.

I grab my book, content to keep my head down, when Evan Moore slides up to my desk. "Hey Abby, want to be partners?"

Gulp.

Evan smiles that gorgeous smile of his, tossing back the bangs of his blondish hair. Suddenly my mind turns to mush. I can't help but smile back at him. "Um, okay, sure."

"Cool." He slides up to my desk and I tell myself it's no big deal, even as my heart flutters and my face goes hot.

"So," he says, fixing the collar of his Polo shirt. His cheeks have two perfect pinkish clusters that remind me of a colorful haze in the cosmos. I'm thinking about my telescope when he nudges my arm. "Abby?"

I blink myself back to the real world. I need to get a grip. What's wrong with me? "Huh? Oh, sorry."

"So, what obstacles do you think Helen Keller faced, being mute and all?"

His question helps me focus. I flip through the book, relishing the smell of the pages. The words flash before my eyes and relax me. "Well, the obstacles were clear. However, she was extremely intelligent and a fast learner. She mastered braille and the typewriter by age ten. She quickly learned the fingertip alphabet and..."

I prattle on, bolstered by Evan's dimply smile. I even jot down the notes for our think-share. In fact, I'm about two pages into a highly-detailed outline when I realize Evan is laughing with Joey and Ryan. Miss Crawford asks him not to prop his feet up on his desk.

My pen stops, I squint my eyes. Cute or not, I know when I'm being used. But then he looks at me and smiles. Again, I smile back. Ugh, I'm so weak. But Evan Moore asked *me* to be his partner. *Fine.* I continue to jot notes as he and his friends go on about poor old Chaz. "Yeah, I heard it's some sort of allergic reaction?"

"Dude, no it's not. It's a terminal disease."

I snort and Evan looks over to me. "Hey Abby, what do you think?"

I look into his dazzling blue eyes. He really does have a smile that can melt ice. I shrug, looking away so I can think. "He's going to be okay. Probably just food poisoning."

Joe scoffs. "Trust me, I saw the guy—so NOT food poisoning. And what was up with Mr. Wolff this morning? Talk about a jackass. Something strange is happening at this school. I'm not so sure we should be here."

From there, the regular rumors fall over the classroom.

Biological warfare

The school was built on a nuclear dump site

We'll all have glowing dots by the end of the year

I keep my head down, plugging along until I've nearly penned a book on nearly everything there is to know about Helen Keller. The whole time, Evan talks, about sports and music and stupid TV shows that I can hardly believe exist. He doesn't notice me again until the bell rings and he looks over my work with a nod.

"Hey, good job, Abby. We're sure to get an A on this thing."

And with a pat on the back, he goes rushing off to his friends, laughing and picking up where they left off during class. I look down at my notes, the painstaking neat handwriting, categorized into neat sections for easy access. A deep sigh. I click my pen closed.

Suddenly, Evan Moore isn't so adorable anymore.

That afternoon, I stop by the field to watch Colton's game. Well, maybe not watch, Colton doesn't exactly play anymore. He's more like a player/coach than anything else. Though I have to say, it was probably the best thing that came out of his epic collapse last year, from benchwarmer to superstar then back to benchwarmer, everyone saw his football IQ.

I'll give him that much, he knows the plays back and forth.

He just can't *make* said plays. But Coach Jackson loves Colton, they've been through a lot together. And so when Colton announced his early retirement, Coach Jackson knew he'd make an excellent assistant coach.

Colton nods along, clapping and encouraging his team, consulting his clipboard. I smile. Being outside makes me feel better about the day. As long as things don't go off the rails like last year, I think I'll be okay. While I, on the other hand, will remain extra vigilant, but lay low, plot and plan more carefully.

I watch my brother do his thing, call the formations and do all the silly hand gestures. I remind myself of what happened to him last year, the hole he'd dug himself when he'd agreed to take part in that New Faces theater production in hopes of winning Lani Andrews' attention. And boy did he get attention as the fairy in *Gypsies and Fairies*, tumbling all over the place. And so I took his props—wand, wings and glitter—and cast a spell. Or at least I thought it was a spell. But after the assembly thing with Mr. Wolff, where I sort of spiraled out of control, I have to admit, I'm a little unnerved about what I'm capable of doing.

And if Colton keeps playing Mr. Responsible, I won't have anyone to discuss it with.

Still, I refuse to admit my brother is actually right about something for once. That maybe I shouldn't be such a vigilante, for lack of a better term. But it's not that easy. I can't simply sit back and let the Chaz Sneads and Reagan Roebucks of the world bully their way through middle school.

What if someone like that became president?

I sit in the stands, trying to watch the game but instead looking over the people walking the track, scrolling through their phones in the bleachers, cheering and clapping and otherwise going on with their daily lives. And there's Reagan Roebuck with her friends, plopping down in the front row, throwing back their hair, all teeth and chewing gum, smiling those mean smiles they've perfected. It isn't long before Evan Moore and the rest of the football team notice them and start laughing and puffing out their chests. They're basically drooling.

It's so frustrating to watch. Soon enough I'm thinking bad thoughts. Really bad things. I feel a tingle, and I know what's coming next. I gather my bags and head out before I cause any more trouble.

The plan for Reagan, Target #3, will happen. But it can't happen right now. I need patience. I have to pick and choose more carefully. Because this morning was out of control.

And if I can't even trust myself, what else do I have?

Chapter 5

I'm three steps into my walk home when Jada Johnson appears out of nowhere. Actually, I think she was hiding in the bushes. Either way, I'm momentarily too stunned to do anything other than stand and gawk.

"Abby, how are you?"

"Hi, Jada."

Jada is always so put together. Her black hair, so severely pulled back, shines in the afternoon sun, although the turtleneck, leather jacket and black pants are a bit much. She looks more the part of cat burglar than focused and determined reporter. Still, despite what Colton says about her motives, I can't help my glowing admiration.

"Seems there's a lot going on around here lately." Ever so discreetly she presses a button on her phone. Gulp.

I kick a pebble with my shoe. "Yeah."

"Are you still writing for the news?"

"Oh um, no. Well, I was, but I have chess and debate, and... spelling." It's hard to even say.

"Yeah, tough break last year."

I keep telling myself she's only buttering me up. But truth is, Jada doesn't work like that, and I'd like to think she sees me as an equal. Last year when she took me under her wing Colton thought it was just to get the scoop on him. But Jada has a softer side only a few get to see.

"How's high school?" I say to change the subject.

She shrugs, then nods with a smile. "Oh, you know. More stories. More *drama*," she says, nudging me with her shoulder. "But I'm more interested in what's going on here. I heard there was another um, event this morning. Something with Mr. Wolff?"

"Yeah," I laugh, shake my head like it's nothing. "Just some foolishness, I think."

In a blink the smile is gone and she's all business again. "Oh, I think it's a lot more than that. First with the mysterious illness, and then from pictures I was sent, they must have spent a fortune on costume design."

"Costume design? *Ha*." Jada turns to face me and I try to pull it together. "I mean, oh, that makes sense."

Her reporter gaze lingers on me a beat too long. Then she nods toward the walkway to the school. "Well hey, I gotta run. Trying to catch Mrs. Tony so I can get the scoop. Talk later?"

The scoop. Oh boy. I can just hear Colton telling me to get far, far away. But it feels good to have someone actually paying attention to me, treating me like a peer and not a little girl. I try to match her confidence, to hold her intense gaze. "Yeah, sure."

The half mile walk home helps clear my mind. And with each step, the wild school day begins to loosen its grip. From Mr. Wolff to Reagan, even the partnership with Evan fades as I hash out equations and formulas in my head. I think about Colton, about Jada. About last year when she suspected something sinister after Colton started lighting up the scoreboard on the field, but I never said a word then and I won't now. Besides, Jada's not onto me. How could she be?

By the time I get down my street and start down the path through our yard toward my house, I'm sort of in a daze. Only the sound of Max barking like a maniac in the window keeps me anchored to the real world.

"Um. Hi, sweetie. Could you give me a hand?"

My father's voice jolts me back into reality. I look left, right, then up where I find him dangling from a limb of the large maple tree in the middle of our yard. He must be nearly twenty feet high, missing a shoe, and his pants are ripped halfway up the seam of the right leg.

"Dad. How?"

He looks down to me with a pleading smile, his voice shaky. "Um," he laughs unsteadily. "Kind of a funny story, really."

When it comes to my father, and Colton for that matter, it's best not to ask how or why. I spot the ladder laying on the ground. "Okay, stay right there," I say, shaking my head as I drop my book bag and rush to grab it.

"Uh oh!"

I spin around and look up. Dad is losing his grip, hanging precariously by one hand. "Sweetie!"

He swings his free arm up for a better hold but his other hand slips. Hanging by his fingers, it's clear he's about to break his neck. Forget the ladder. "Dad!"

He calls out as his grip gives way. "Arggh!"

I gasp, tingle, and slow my Dad's plummet to a float.

He's still screaming as I gently set him down in a pile of leaves. He settles with an *oomph*, and leaves go flying as he spins, rolls, then leaps to his feet. His eyes widen with his smile as he realizes he's not dead, and he looks around wildly, shaking out his arms and legs, rolling his neck and muttering to himself. His hair is full of leaves.

"What in the..." His head swivels. He looks up, down, right then left. He pats himself down, stammering and wobbly as he feels around his back, looking for wings for all I can tell. When he sees me, his eyes go even wider. "Abby! Did you...did you *see* that?"

See it? *I did it.*

"Um, yes. That was close, Dad. You have to be more careful." I try to downplay it, start for the door. Not happening.

"Close? Abby, that was amazing." He comes storming up to me, his eyes like pinwheels. He shoots a glance back to the limb and laughs. "It's unbelievable, like..." He wipes his brow. He's all over the place, glancing down the tree to the pile of leaves I set him in. "It was some sort of, of..."

I wince as he closes the space between us and takes me by the shoulders. It's over. My big secret is out. My parents will ship me off, and I'll end up in a roadside carnival. But as he looks me in the eyes, his face sort of crazed, his smile at a tilt, I realize he doesn't suspect me. It's worse. He thinks it's...

"Abby, that was nothing short of a real-life miracle."

Oh boy.

"Or... I don't know. Gosh, maybe it was...maybe it was something *supernatural*."

Oh boy again.

Dad paces the yard with his hand to his chin. He looks to the maple, then to the scattered leaf pile where he landed. He spreads his hands before his face, wiggling his fingers.

"I could have superpowers. I mean, I've heard of these things happening. Like a mother holding up a car so her children could rush out unharmed, or a man falling from a plane, landing without a scratch." He bites his lip, a sure sign he's plotting one of his *big ideas*. Then he gazes out to the driveway, maybe searching for witnesses. "Wait until your mother hears about this."

I try to deflect, change the subject, even as I know it's no use. "How long were you up there, Dad?"

He scratches his head. "It's hard to say. I was trying to get that broken limb down." He looks up. "Thing's been bothering me for months. I thought I could do it before Colton's game but...the ladder fell." He shoots me a look. "Ah man, I missed the game. Well, you hungry? We need to get to Michelangelo's."

The football team meets up at Michelangelo's for pizza after every game. I was looking forward to the quiet time. All I've been wanting to do is sit in my room and sulk, but now I'm thinking it's a good opportunity to talk Dad down on the way over. I try not to think about Colton and what he'll say once he hears. Sheesh. If only this day could end.

But it's no use. We get cleaned up, but Dad can hardly drive as he goes on about miracles. And he's no less worked up as we park and he sort of runs/hobbles to the door while I gently remind him we should probably let Colton have the spotlight. Walking in, some parents grab a table and announce the Panthers won. Dad nods, says how great it is that they won, but I can tell by the starry look in his eyes it's only a matter of time before he spills what he's already titled, "The Miracle on Berkshire Street."

Colton and some of his teammates are loud and obnoxious in the middle of the restaurant, where they've pushed two tables together. Mom waves us over, and I sigh because this day has no end in sight. All I want to do is curl up and read a book.

Mom gives Dad the once over. He's changed pants but still looks like a man who's been swimming in a leaf pile. I reach to grab the one out from behind his ear, but he's too tall and he can't stay still. Mom turns to me for answers. But I can only shrug. Then she asks him directly. "Honey, what happened?"

As I've said, Dad and Colton are always having mishaps, so it takes a lot for my mom to ask this question. And with it goes any hopes of keeping it under Colton's radar.

Sure enough, Colton saunters over. Dad throws an arm around him. "There you are, son. Wow, what a game, so I heard. Sorry I missed it. Really, but listen, so I was on the ladder, and—"

Mom sets her water down. "Rob, I thought we talked about this. You shouldn't be on a ladder when no one is home. Did you at least let Mrs. Bouchard know, so she could watch from her window? She could've called for help."

Again, it's no secret about my dad and accidents, they're sort of on a BFF basis. Dad waves Mom off. "No need to bother the fire department again. Besides," he says looking to me. "That's not even the cool part, is it Abby?"

So much for lying low. Before I can respond, Colton wedges his way into things. He shoots me a look. "Yeah, so what happened, Dad?"

My father's smile doubles. Some of the football guys wander over, and he welcomes the crowd. "So, I was pruning the tree," he begins, as though he's settling in for some campfire tale, "when the ladder tips over. I must have been stuck there dangling for hours, most of the day, really. Right, sweetheart?"

Oh boy. My dad has been known to embellish a story. Minutes turn to hours, hours into days. So now, as everyone turns to me, all I can do is shrug. "Well, I can't say, Dad."

He shakes his head. "Hmm, yeah, since around lunch. And then, just when Abby came home, well, tell you what...boy am I glad you showed up. Now I have a witness. This is absolutely unreal, totally unbelievable. You're never going to believe this."

Colton cocks his head, still staring at me. "Yeah, try me."

I point to a waiter. "Oh look, here comes our pizza. Um, so I have to use the bathroom. Back in a sec."

I get two steps before Colton sets his hand on my shoulder. "Whoa now, I'm sure it can wait. I mean, we're all dying to hear this wild story. And, *you were there,* right?"

"Well, I..." I want to stomp his foot.

Dad laughs. "Yes, hang on, sweetie, Colton's right. Back me up on this. Okay, so I'm hanging from this limb..."

The pizza arrives, but my appetite has left the building. How can I eat with Colton glaring at me as Dad goes on with a slow-mo recap of everything? Dad builds to the pause in the air, the slowing, the floating, and the landing "light as a feather."

Some of the football guys laugh. It sounds crazy because it is crazy. And Dad isn't helping, calling it a *tried-and-true, once-in-a-lifetime experience.* By this point, I'm doing my best to avoid Colton's eyes. And for a while it's working, maybe, kinda, until Phillip Jenkins opens his fat mouth.

"Mr. Clutts, that's so weird. You know, this morning, Mr. Wolff, our new principal, the guy turned into a donkey right in front of the whole school."

The football players fold over in laughter. Then everyone's talking about the assembly, how the school pulled off such an elaborate prank. They're braying and whinnying and having a good time. All but Colton, of course.

Dad, looking wounded after losing the spotlight, shrugs. "Well, that is strange, I suppose."

Phillip laughs. "Strange isn't the word for it. Our principal grew a tail!"

"And ears," someone adds.

"And hoofs," comes another voice. "He was like a piñata out there."

The team tightens around our table, talking fast and loud about our principal while Colton gives me that smug, *see-what-you've-done* smirk he's so fond of.

The donkey.

No, it was a mule!

A Clydesdale!

Phillip grabs a triangle of pizza. The team digs in, and I study the shapes and angles as the pie is divided. But before I can make a pi joke, Phillip tears into the last slice and keeps on talking through a mouthful. "Whatever it was, it was the craziest thing I've ever seen. People are saying it was a gag, but man, they must have hired a special effects crew, it was so real."

Dad finally finds that leaf behind his ear. He looks it over. "Well, I certainly don't think tax payers should have to foot the bill for that."

"Maybe not," Phillip adds. "But. it was lit. He looked like something from Space Farm."

Dad stirs his tea. "Lit, huh. Space Farm? Is that a movie?"

"It's an app."

"Oh. Right."

Another pie arrives and Phillip doesn't miss a beat getting another slice. "Anyway, on top of what happened with Chaz Snead, things are getting weird around Peakland, really weird."

Annnd there's my cue to get out of there. I manage to slip back a few steps. "I really have to use the—"

Once again Colton blocks my path. "Abby, are you okay? You don't look so hot."

"Well, she did see her father float out of a tree," Dad says, steering the conversation back to his big event. Mom is up in an instant. She sets a cheek to my forehead, wipes my hair back. I would be mortified if it weren't for everything else.

But something about how she looks me over is different. Her eyes are like scanners, vivid and alert. I'm about to ask what she's doing when she stops.

"You do feel warm," she says.

Phillip eases away, as though all his suspicions are confirmed. "Covid-22. Told you."

I'm not worried about Phillip Jenkins' phony science but my brother, who won't quit it with the smirk. And whatever Mom was doing with her eyes.

When did this happen? When did Colt become the

responsible one? Last year, when he was always finding a way to flub things up, it was me who bailed him out.

Now, as Mom leads me to the bathroom, it's clear my brother and I are going to have another little chat. And soon.

Chapter 6

Colton paces my room. "You've gone too far, Abby. Completely too far."

He peeks in my closet—a blatant invasion of privacy—then examines the windowsill where the quartz stones are arranged in a certain way in accordance to the waxing moon's activity.

"Hey, leave those there. And what was I supposed to do, let Dad fall and break his neck?"

He turns from the window. "This isn't about Dad. It's about turning our principal into a donkey."

Giggle city. I know he thinks he's intimidating, but it's not his style. It doesn't help that he's wearing his baggy pajama sweatpants with one of those ridiculous, *Colt the Bolt* t-shirts. We have boxes of them in the basement leftover from his brief time as a superstar. Dad uses one as a shammy when he washes the car.

Colton crosses his arms, doing his best to push out his muscles. "Talk. Because I'm this close to going to Mom."

My jaw drops. "You wouldn't. And it is about Dad. He's telling the whole world about it."

He cocks his head. "No? Try me."

Wow. I liked him better when he was a human wrecking ball. Now, as a big time eighth grader, he's entirely too bossy. "Okay, two things. The Mr. Wolff incident was an accident. I mean, he was on my list, but..."

Colton pounces. "*List?* You have a list? And what do you mean, *accident*, or *incident*? I suppose that sounds better than *cast a spell on my principal*."

I scoot to the edge of the bed. "But that's just it. I didn't exactly cast a spell. I didn't even mean to do it. I don't think... I mean, it wasn't on purpose."

Colton drops his tough guy act. He takes a seat. "Wait, hang on. What do you mean, it wasn't a spell?"

"Well, I..." I look to my floor, then to the window, down to my bedspread. "It's hard to explain. And you can't get upset with me."

Colton looks me over, nodding. He actually seems more interested than upset. "Okay, I won't. I'll try not to. But you need to tell me everything."

There's not much to hide with my brother, not after last year when he and Zach forced me to create more spells after they realized the ones I did on his fairy props worked. So I tell him about my targeting system, the planned spells. He slows me down when I start talking fast. His eyes go big when I explain the assembly thing with Mr. Wolff, then finding Dad in the tree —which, normally wouldn't be a big deal until the part about how I sort of floated him down to safety.

For the most part, he listens, only interrupting to ask about the tingles on my scalp right before Mr. Wolff's nose grew.

"Yeah, I don't know. I was...upset. He was up there grandstanding and something about it really got under my skin."

"I'll say." Colton smiles. And it's like the old Colton smile I've missed so much. "But I mean, Abby, you sort of have super powers."

I toss my hands in my lap. "Oh my gosh. You sound like Dad. Besides, I don't feel so super. I feel, a little terrified." I shrug. "I need to get this under control before I end up in a lab somewhere. You can't say anything. This has to stay a secret while I research."

"Relax. Your secret is safe."

I shoot him a look. "I mean it, Colton. Not even big mouth Zach."

He holds his hands up. "Okay, okay."

We sit there for a minute, taking it in. It's not every day you turn your principal into a donkey. Then Colton slaps his knees, gets to his feet, and smiles. He points to a cup sitting on my desk. "Okay, sis. Make it fly."

I cock my head at him. "Um. What?"

Colton nods to the cup again, still with that goofy grin on his face. "The cup, make it fly."

I roll my eyes, but now with a smile. "I'm not, no. Like I said, I'm not sure how it works."

"Blink your eyes, like, wrinkle up your nose and..." He blinks, wrinkles, and nods toward the cup. The only thing that moves is the hair on his head.

"Is that from that silly old show Grandpa watches?'

He shrugs. "I don't know. Try this." He snaps his fingers. "I hereby command you to moooove."

"What am I, a carnival attraction?"

"You know what?"

"What?"

We both jump as Dad pokes his head in the door. "There you are. I was wondering where the two of you went. What's going on?"

"Going on? Nothing." I glance at the cup. *Don't move it. Don't move it. Don't move it.*

A grin breaks across my dad's face. Clearly he hasn't let the floating thing go just yet. "So, I um, I was thinking about earlier. I'm going to write up an account of everything. Abby, I might need your help. Not tonight, or anything, I'm going to brainstorm. But I really think we've got something, one of those supernatural occurrences."

I cut a look to Colton, then to my dad who's staring at his hands as though they were gold blocks. "Dad, it wasn't really supernatural."

He opens the door wider. "Abby, what do you mean? It was... I was floating. Suspended in the air. I mean, you saw me. You were there."

Colton turns to me with a grin, obviously enjoying my misery.

I take a more delicate approach. "What if it's just the way we remember it? Like, time slows down when something happens, you know?"

Dad shakes me off. "Sweetheart, I've taken my share of falls in my lifetime, and today was something different." He yawns, his body unable to keep up with his brain. "Well, okay, I'm beat. Going to bed. Flying takes a lot of energy, you know?"

He pulls the door shut. Colton smirks at me. "He's never going to let this go."

"Yeah, I know. But seriously, what was I supposed to do, let him crack his head open?"

"Well, so much for keeping this thing a secret. He's brainstorming."

We both giggle. "Hope he doesn't hurt himself."

Colton gets to his feet. "Well, I've got to go study."

"I'm sorry, did you just say you have to go study?"

He smiles. "I bet Lani that I could make honor roll."

I laugh. "Wow, and people think *I'm* the nerd around here."

"Haha. But... Abby, please try to stay out of trouble," he says. "Man, never thought I'd be saying this, but just, I don't know. Lay low for a few days. No um, targets. Got it?"

"Got it."

"Cool."

He pulls the door shut behind him. And I sit there on my bed wondering how my life became so strange that it's hardly real anymore. I mean, Colton studying, going for honor roll, telling *me* to lay low. Chaz, Mr. Wolff, Dad, I have to slow down. I do. But...

I turn to the desk where Colton left the cup. I tilt my head and the cup tips one way then the other before I nod my head and it takes flight.

I hold it there, eye level, hovering. I make it zip left, right, then flip it over. It does circles around my room. I go up, down, let it fall then catch it again with my eyes.

Easy. With the cup still in the air, I lift one of my book bags and unzip it. The Helen Keller book joins the cup, its pages fluttering as I add a textbook. Soon everything is floating, the cup, the bag, the books, pages and pages of words to spell. I even hurl my wastebasket into the debris for good measure. I watch the orbit, my own private galaxy. I add a few more books, then my favorite pair of tennis shoes. Soon, my room is full of floating debris, and I'm both fascinated and terrified at the same time.

Ugh, what a freak.

With a sigh, I shrug and everything falls to the floor. I look at the light switch, stick out my tongue and all goes dark. I fall back in bed, my skin tingling, breaths shaky, my mind roaming through theorems, right triangle formulas, pizza slices, and equilateral triangle points, of all things. *Wow*, I think, shaking it off. *I really need a life.*

I close my eyes and think about cute boys like Evan Moore and pretty girls like Reagan Roebuck. What makes them special, popular, normal?

It's clear I'll never be any of those things.

Chapter 7

WERG runs a story on Saturday about the "odd string of events" recently at Peakland Middle School. It begins with an in-depth (one-sided) look at Chaz and his mysterious illness before jumping to the several eyewitness accounts of what took place with Mr. Wolff in the gym before concluding with a grave warning about these several, "unconfirmed incidents" taking place.

Under normal circumstances, I'd be laughing at the hack job reporting, but the story mentioned how recordings are being analyzed *as we speak*. And it's with that in mind that I flip on the laptop to have a look for myself.

I find ten videos posted to YouTube, half of them crystal clear, showing Mr. Wolff morphing into a donkey. The only thing that keeps me from hyperventilating is how cynical people are. Determined not to be gullible, everyone refuses to believe what they are seeing.

Hoax.

Farce.

Nice Try

Fakest thing I've ever seen.

I slap the laptop shut and sit back with a smile. No one believes anything anymore. We've been fooled too many times. This, combined with all the middle school gossip, is the kind of skepticism a girl like me can depend on.

Take, for example, a quote from Jackson Palma: "Yeah, like, the teachers are all aliens. I knew it all along. I don't feel safe here, and I don't think I can do any homework for a week."

That's right, Jackson. Keep 'em coming.

So while the news is diligently reporting the story, I assure Colton all is fine. Because even HD proof of our principal morphing into a donkey is swiftly debunked, and by Monday things at Peakland Middle are status quo. And since nothing is out of place on campus and all tests clear Mr. Wolff and Chaz, medically speaking, of any harm, it leaves the town divided. There are those who scoff at such elaborate pranks, and those who fully believe in the comic book conspiracy theories.

That said, I did not factor in the resiliency of the jerk chromosome. The way Chaz Snead guns for the camera, how he's all too pleased with himself, happy to soak up all the attention like a chump, has me grinding my teeth. He makes it abundantly clear he's feeling fine, bragging about how it's going to take a lot more than some aliens or some government experiment to bring him down. He plans on returning to school at full strength on Monday. He's glad to play the role of hero, having battled back and fended off whatever plagued him. I should've turned him green for a year.

And Mr. Wolff has a lot to say as well. In his interview with WERG he's clever and glib about the donkey incident. By refusing to confirm nor deny he was in on the prank, he laughs it off, no comment except that he expects a regular schedule on Monday. It's clear he wants people to believe maybe he was behind the whole thing. He's even written an editorial to *The Times*, our local newspaper. It's maddening. I should've left him with hooves.

Dad lays the paper down. "That new principal is really something."

I'm about to make a joke about it when I spot Mom's

planner on the table. She still uses good old fashioned pen and pad. But it's what she's scribbled down that grabs my attention.

Abby – Piedmont School. Tues?

"What's this?"

"Oh." Mom looks at Dad, who nearly knocks his cereal bowl to the floor.

"Yeah, er, that's a, remember we discussed maybe visiting with the Piedmont School?"

"Um no, I don't. I think I would've remembered that."

Poor Dad, perched and helpless in his chair, waiting for a sign on how to handle this. Gosh, it's so easy to figure them out. Mom is the boss and Dad does his best to remain relevant when it comes to family decisions.

Sure enough, Mom clears her throat and dives into the spiel. "Sweetheart, we need to think about expanding your options."

"Wait." I turn to Dad, who squirms like he's out on a limb again. "Were you going to bother to tell me about this?"

Dad looks at Mom, then, like a parrot, gives me the same line. "Abby, your mother and I just thought we'd visit, see what sort of opportunities they have available. It's not even a real scho—"

"Don't you want..." Mom edges her way into the dining room. "Don't you want to see what else is out there? I mean, you've already skipped a grade, what else can Peakland offer? And besides, it's only something I was mulling over. It's not written in stone."

Her voice is weird. I roll my neck because it feels tight. Are they serious? They want to ship me off to private school? No way. Time to end this now and forever. "Well, for one, it's good enough for Colton."

My parents have always been careful when it comes to my brother and me. They'd never want to show favoritism by sending their daughter to some swanky private school while leaving Colton to tough it out in remedial city.

Sure enough, it works. Mom grabs her planner and stashes it in her purse. "I was only planning a visit. Nothing more."

I wave her off. "I don't want to go to the Piedmont, whatever it's called. I want to do the spelling bee, go to Nationals." I turn to Dad. "And what do you mean 'it's not a real school'?"

Dad shrugs. "It's not, I couldn't find a single thing on it. It's like it's..."

"It's highly selective." Mom's voice is stern, aimed at my father. She redirects. "And again, we just thought it might be nice to explore..."

Wow. It's taken me this long to get used to school. Now, with my targets being neutralized and the school spelling rounds coming up, I'm finally on my path to redemption. And they want to send me off? They can't. They just can't.

A quick tingle and Dad's bowl trembles. He catches it, grips his spoon, and looks it over. I clench my fists to keep from losing it. Mom's eyes are wide as she comes to my side. "Abby, settle down."

"We talked about this. You said I could go to Peakland." Mom rubs my shoulders. Dad holds up the bowl, inspects the bottom. "I can't believe you guys are plotting behind my back like this."

"Honey, we're not plotting anything," Mom says. I guess she didn't notice the bowl thing. "We're only trying to help you reach your..."

"*Potential*. Yeah, I got that. Do you guys have a script or something?"

I take a few deep breaths as the tingles rise up again to my neck and the back of my head. I know I'm being a snot, but I can't help myself. I look away from Dad's bowl to the window, but then that shakes too. I close my eyes as Dad gets to his feet to investigate while Mom only watches me with something like...what? Pride. Then she's back, rubbing shoulders. It works. My body relaxes. I sit down again.

"Abby. You're a gifted young lady. But you seem bored at Peakland Middle School. There is no challenge for you. Sweetheart, you're breezing through."

"Yeah? What about my epic collapse on stage in the Nationals? How was that for breezing through?"

"Abby, you were a *national* finalist. It was an extraordinary—"

"Embarrassing, is what it was. E-M-B-A-R-R-A-S-S-I-N-G. You know, the word should've been 'mortifying'."

Dad smiles, still with a palm on the window. "Think of it this way. You'll never misspell it again, that's for sure. Learn from your mistakes, that's my motto."

My dad, such a lovable oaf. But there are other reasons I want to stay at Peakland. Yes, the spelling bee. I do want redemption. But if I go off to a new school, who will protect Chucky and Ahmad from the likes of Chaz and Reagan? I can't believe they—no, not they, Mom—wants to pull this. I shoot her my best pout.

"Is this like a boarding school? Are you guys trying to ship me off?"

"Oh Abby, no one is shipping you off. You would be a day kid."

I take a breath, easing the tingles down my spine. Deep breaths. I guess it wouldn't hurt to appease them, get them off my back, quite literally. Even if I have no intentions of going to some stupid private boarding school. "Okay, I'll go, just to take the tour, nothing else."

Mom surprises me with a hug. "Oh great, sweetie. And don't worry, you can still do the bee."

Satisfied with the window, Dad comes plodding back over.

"And hey, look at it this way, it would get you away from that strange principal. What sort of name is Kaspar, anyway?"

Mom breaks away. "What did you say?"

Dad gestures to the paper. "The new guy, the principal. Oh, that's right, you weren't there for orientation. The guy's one weird dude, isn't he, Abby?"

Mom sets a hand to her forehead. She stares at Dad. "You never told me...that."

Dad looks around, probably wondering what he did to get in trouble. "What, the school thing? You were showing a house, I took the kids, remember?"

Mom's face goes pale. She shakes her head. "I knew something was off, but you never said..." She plops onto the couch, muttering "Kaspar" under her breath.

"Are you okay, Mom?"

"Yeah. I..." She wipes at her lap, then nods a few times to herself before she smiles at me. "Gosh, I'm a terrible mother."

I shoot Dad a look. "Mom, no you're not."

Dad swoops in for the rescue. "Yeah, it was nothing. It was what, an hour, tops, right Abby?"

"Yeah, it was nothing."

Mom nods along, then looks at me again. "I would really like you to take this tour, Abby."

Dad takes his place beside Mom, scoops up her hand. Something stinks around here. What's her deal? It's like the name Kaspar spooked her. Does she know something about him? No, she couldn't. Mr. Wolff isn't even from Peakland, and his accent has some quirks but I've narrowed it down to somewhere along the lines of Swiss German. Hmm, I'll have to dig deeper into this Kaspar thing.

With Dad consoling Mom, I slowly back away. "Okay, well, I'm going to my room to rest."

And they don't even try to stop me. They don't say, "on a

Saturday morning?" Which lets me know right then strange things are happening. Stranger than cups floating or green-skinned bullies. Dad acting weird? Sure, we're used to that. But Mom, getting so flustered. The back rubs. This talk about shipping me off.

Nope, she knows something and I need to find out what it is, and fast, before I end up at the Piedmont School—whatever that is—wearing plaid skirts and knee socks, getting brainwashed.

Chapter 8

The next morning begins like any other: kids shuffling off the bus, getting dropped off by parents, people meeting in the lobby where the murmur of conversations float across the worn polished floors. The occasional laughter breaks from the groups. The cool kids, the jocks, the nerds, the loners. In-between-kids. All in their tight knit circles.

I'm at our normal spot, past the benches that line the wall near the fire extinguisher, looking out for Chucky and Ahmad, wishing they would show up and distract me and my thoughts. I should be studying my spelling list, but I can't focus on that. I'm not in the greatest mood. Between the news and the Piedmont talk I'm still broiling angry. The more I think about it the worse it gets.

And I'm simmering when Target #3 comes sashaying down the hallway.

Yes, I told myself I was going to back off, let things cool down before resuming the plan. I mean, the threat of private school is firmly on the table. And yet, one look at Reagan Roebuck flouncing down the hallway minutes before the bell, and the tingling sweeps down my back.

I'm no longer steering the ship. And oh boy, bad things are coming.

Reagan pivots to a stop in the middle of the lobby, her head cocked, her sky blue eyes glimmering with malice as she scans potential victims. She'll go after a heavy girl or maybe someone not up to date on their fashion sense. Colton defends her sometimes because again, she is pretty, I'll give her that. But she's not pretty on the inside, trust me; she's ugly as rust. Perhaps today is the day to make it all match.

She flashes a grin to her followers, flings her laugh like a weapon. Her perfect hair shines as she throws her head back as the less fortunate are left hoping it isn't their lucky morning. What kills me is how they all wish they could be her. But not me. Not anymore.

She whispers to Jordan and Jordan whispers to Hailey as the world's funniest secret is spread. I slink back into my corner, not out of fear, although part of me still hopes she'll change her mind and go strutting off before it's too late, then everything might work itself out.

No such luck. Another round of whispering, and her eyes narrow with that *ha-ha-ha*, high-pitched chortle designed to make other girls shudder. She locks in on Jennifer Calloway—an eighth grader, one of the nicest girls in my geometry class. We all know what's coming next, and poor Jennifer knows it too as she backs into a corner, dropping her gaze to the floor like she wishes she could bury herself in it. I can't let this happen. I *won't* let this happen. And so when Reagan swoops in on her prey, it's time to act.

It starts with her mouth. For a girl so pretty she has the most irritating voice I've ever heard. It's a grating, high pitched whine, and it doesn't help that everything she says—a string of fragments, slang, and lazy grammar—is intended to hurt someone's feelings.

Miss Spell Girl, huh? I'll show her. The tingles shoot up my back to my neck. My brain winks, fires, and Reagan's perfect, unblemished chin becomes a thing of the past.

I take a step forward out of no-man's-land toward the

middle of the lobby. I narrow my eyes on Reagan, who, having belittled poor Jennifer, is still laughing as she turns to Jordan. Jordan's smile plummets. Her eyes widen, and she slaps a hand over her mouth. Another round of tingles in my head, and everyone goes quiet as it grows—a wart the size of a lima bean on Reagan's chin.

Jordan's eyes double in size as she leans closer. Hailey jerks away with a shriek. Reagan's laugh stops on a dime. Her brow wrinkles. She looks left, then right, probably wondering why everyone is not cowering but gawking. Again she turns to her flunkies and asks what's going on, when Jordan apparently informs her about the h-u-m-o-n-g-o-u-s growth on her face. With a shrug, I give old Reagan another one on her cheek, and *oh why not?* Another on her forehead.

I can't help my giggles, and I can't stop there. When Reagan's hand flies to her face, I bite my lip and—oops!—three coarse hairs pop out of the wart on her chin.

Reagan lets go with a scream that could wake the dead. For these girls, looks are everything—life or death—and so a wart on the face is terminal. Reagan's book bag hits the floor like an anvil as she sprints to the girls' bathroom. The entire lobby watches as she breaks all track and field records in the one-hundred-yard dash.

Another piercing scream ruptures from inside the bathroom as she finds—let me count—not one, or two, but a dozen ghastly warts congregating on her lovely face.

Oh, Reagan, don't worry. They'll be gone tomorrow, and hopefully you will be better for it.

But what's another wart? And more black, stringy hairs in the center? Another tingle, another shriek from the bathroom.

Chucky and Ahmad arrive as the hallways are buzzing with theories. Jordan wheels around, feeling her own face as she cautiously approaches the bathroom. Hailey has tears streaming down her cheeks. People shake their heads, recounting the story, as Reagan's wails boom through the school.

"What did we miss?"

I turn to Chucky. "The fall of the queen."

Ahmad looks at Chucky, who looks at me with a suspicious eye. "Why do I get the feeling you know something you're not telling me?"

I shrug and pat Chucky on the head. "Girl stuff."

With that, I skip off to first period.

By third period the entire school has heard the news: Beautiful Reagan Roebuck is covered with more warts than a landfill toad. The rumors crank up. She's contracted a rare skin condition. Another allergic reaction. And it doesn't take long to link it to Chaz Snead or Mr. Wolff.

Mrs. Tony conducts an emergency broadcast to let the school know that, despite the odd occurrences as of late, Peakland Middle is completely safe. Meanwhile, Reagan has left the school. The warts have done her in, and for someone as vain as Reagan Roebuck, it's more than she can take.

So yeah, people are talking. Even Chucky is putting things together. My parents want to ship me off to a school that may or may not exist, and I haven't studied a lick for my spelling bee today. But you know what? Peakland Middle is down three bullies.

Things could be worse.

Chapter 9

I hit the library at lunch in an effort to avoid Colton. Not a daunting task, as I'm not sure he's even aware the library has a resource room. But I can't take chances, I keep my head down and manage to lock myself away. I get out of my routine. I take new routes to class. It works, I manage to get through the day without turning anyone into a beetle. And by the time the final bell rings, I'm feeling awfully good about myself. At least until I walk outside and find Mom's van at the curb.

With all my planning, I totally forgot she was picking us up for dental checkups. Sure enough, Colton's waiting for me at the van. He blocks me from getting in, his new habit these days. But when I look up to meet his gaze it's clear he's more concerned than angry. He grabs the back of his neck. "Please tell me it's not permanent."

I smile, relieved he's not playing parent again. I shake my head. Poor boys. As much of a terror as Reagan Roebuck may be, they can't imagine the thought of her pretty little face being tarnished. But still, he's not giving me a hard time, so I assure him it's temporary.

He breathes a sigh of relief. I laugh. "So, you nervous about tonight?"

Being that Colton holds all Peakland High offensive records, he's expected at every home game. Especially tonight's big clash with Hillsdale.

"No. I mean, well, maybe a little." He shrugs. "Warts though, seriously? So much for lying low, Abby."

I hold my hands up. "I'm all done."

"Really?"

I nod. And this time I mean it. I've neutralized my targets and hopefully the lessons have been learned. Now I can focus on my redemption, the spelling bee. And Colton must believe me because he's doing that goofy smile that reminds me of Dad. Or maybe he's taking it easy on me because he knows about this private school thing Mom and Dad are plotting.

Behind us, someone honks the horn. Mom tells us to get moving. Colton starts to let me in the van, but this time I stop him. "Hey, do you know anything about this Piedmont School Mom is talking about?"

"Huh? Piedmont? Nope, never heard of it."

"Yeah, no one has. And that's what worries me."

Colton raises one eyebrow before he turns and climbs in the van. I look back just in time to catch Mr. Wolff watching me from the school entrance. We stare each other down for five seconds. Ten. Another honk of the horn behind us. Again, Mom tells me to hurry. With that, I tear my gaze away from Mr. Wolff and climb into the van.

Mom is a careful driver. She always puts her signal on with plenty of time to spare. She eyes the rearview and lets others merge. She hums to herself and waves to let others out in front of her. She never texts and drives.

But today she's tapping on the steering wheel, fidgeting with the rearview mirror. She changes radio stations three times before she turns to me with that thoughtful look in her eye. "I heard there was another incident today?"

"Oh?" I say, because my tongue takes a trip down my throat. I don't dare look at Colton. Mom keeps tapping on the wheel.

"It's strange, these occurrences, whatever is going on. Don't you think?"

My brain can't deal. More with that word again. I do the spelling. O-C-C-U-R-R-E-N-C-E-S, before I manage a glance back to Colton, sitting in the back bopping around with his headphones on. "Yeah, I guess."

"I'll say. I mean, first the whole thing with Chaz, then Mr. Wolff, and now Reagan Roebuck."

"Yeah," I say, wondering how she already knows about Reagan. Maybe the school sent out a mass text message.

Mom isn't done. "You were just talking about Chaz and Reagan, remember?"

Gulp. "No, not really."

"Yeah, at dinner. You were saying how Chaz was always picking on your friends." Now she's snapping her fingers, a sure sign she's connecting the dots. "And Reagan, what was it you were saying, she needed to get 'taken down a rung'?"

I slink down in my seat, chance a look at her. She stares straight ahead, at traffic, setting her blinker and waiting to pull in to Triangle Square, where Dr. Rosebud's office is located. Normally I'd joke about the absurd name, but today I'm only hoping there's not a long wait at the office. I'd rather have my teeth cleaned than sit through my mother's polite interrogation. Did Colton rat me out?

Another glance back at him. He shrugs, mumbling along with his music, if you can call it that. Hmm. Back to Mom, craning her head to check the traffic. "Well, I hope you kids are safe, is all. I mean, if something's going around, maybe we should skip the game tonight," she yells over her shoulder, referring to the varsity game.

"What? We can't." Colton rips off his headphones. "Mom, it's the Hillsdale game. I can't miss it. I'm an honorary captain."

It's true, when I made the magic glitter last year and Colton ran wild in Peakland's improbable victory over Hillsdale High, they broke a ten year losing streak. Now, in his early retirement, he's being treated like a good-luck charm. It's why they asked him to come out and give the team a pep talk tonight.

Mom shakes her head at Colton through the rearview mirror. Traffic flies by in both directions as we wait in the center turning lane as Colton throws a fit and they go back and forth. Mom starts to go, easing forward, but sees a car and stops. Then she starts forward again, still explaining to Colton, "I know. But with all the strange happenings at Peak—"

We start to turn. I scream as a truck veers into our lane out of nowhere, barreling down on us. Colton yells, "Mom, look out!"

Ten feet. Five. The blast of a horn. A silent scream leaves my throat as I brace for impact. Then...

Nothing. I blink, wiggle my toes. We haven't smashed to smithereens. The truck sits maybe a few feet away from our bumper. And all four of its tires are off the ground, about a foot in the air.

The driver of the truck, still white knuckling the steering wheel, opens his eyes and looks around. He shuts his eyes tight and tries again. Probably because his truck is floating. I mean *actually* floating, hovering like the cup in my room. Weirder still is how I didn't feel any tingles or even realize I was doing it. One second we're bickering about the game, the next the truck is coming for us. I only had time to brace for impact. Never felt the tingles or the numbness until it was about to smash into us. But there it is, unscathed, the grill right before our eyes.

Mom, with a lock of hair over her face, hardly even seems flustered. She's not even breathing heavy as she looks back to us. "Everyone okay?"

We nod silently. The truck gently returns to the ground. The driver still sits at the wheel, blinking, his mouth moving as he too realizes he's not dead. Mom throws him a wave and pulls into Dr. Rosebud's office like nothing ever happened.

I glance down to my hands, wipe my palms on my legs. Am I really doing this without even knowing it now? Because I didn't even think about it. I was too busy preparing to be roadkill. One second an enormous truck is about to bash into us, the next, time stops and we're completely safe.

And Mom, gathering her things and talking about being late. It's like she hardly noticed. Although her voice is a bit *too* upbeat and positive, like it's forced. She checks the mirror, fixing her hair. Then she leaps out of the car and throws an arm through her pocket book strap. "Okay, let's all take a breath. That was close, people really should pay more attention. Everyone okay?"

Colton and I nod. Mom smiles and turns. "Well, let's get inside. We're running late."

We sit and stare at her. She doesn't notice we're still in the van until she's at the entrance to the dentist office.

"Well, come on," she says. She never even looks out to the street where the man is out of the car, inspecting his truck for wings, far as I can tell. He sees us and wipes his head. But Mom is busy in her own world. Did she not just see a floating truck?

Getting out, Colton only stares at me. Mom yanks the building's door open and motions again for us to hurry along. "Come on, kids. We're running late."

Colton brushes past me. I look back to the street, the truck still out there in the center lane. The guy shakes his head, kicks the tires. Maybe he's wondering if he mistakenly bought the hovercraft edition without knowing it.

Colton sets a hand on my shoulder. "Wow, that was close. Thanks for saving my life, I guess."

I open my mouth but nothing comes out. Colton shakes his head, laughs, and strolls into the waiting room.

Mom, still holding the door, gazes out to the street, refusing to look at me. And it isn't until I'm inside that she blinks, takes a sudden breath, and starts for the counter to check us in. And it's only then I'm able to say the words.

"It wasn't me."

COLTON HAS THREE CAVITIES. I have none because I actually floss. There's an opening and so they go ahead and do the fillings right then and there, which leaves Mom and me in the waiting room, flipping through magazines and pretending nothing is super weird between us. It's exactly as I feared.

I gloss over an article about space clutter in *Popular Mechanics*. Mom buries her nose in a fashion magazine. I can't take it any longer, I need some answers. "That sure was close out there, huh?"

Mom looks up as though she hadn't given our near death experience much thought. "It was," she says with a smile. "It's why I'm such a cautious driver."

"Yeah," I agree, "but..." I set the magazine down. "Mom."

"Yes, dear?"

My mom's eyes sparkle with gentleness. She looks around before she opens her mouth to speak. I'm on the edge of my seat when the door to the back swings open.

We both jump. A scowling dental assistant perp-walks Colton out to the lobby by his collar. Colton's face is flushed and his mouth is lopsided and he's drooling. The dental assistant curls her lips at him, and once she's disposed of Colton she clutches her hand.

One last glare at Colton as he walks to the door with his head down.

Mom leaps up. "Colton?" Then she turns to the dental assistant who shakes her head.

"The little creep bit my hand."

Colton looks back. "I swaid I wuhls sowwy."

I cover my smile. Only Colton. Mom works to smooth things over with the assistant while I try not to laugh at my brother.

"Wow, uh, you better hope that wears off in time for your big pep talk," I say to Colton. His eyes go big. Mom turns back to us, her mouth open with surprise. I laugh. "What, you guys forgot?"

Mom schedules our next check-ups while Colton and I walk out to the van. He's shaking his head, mumbling in some strange, swollen language I can't decipher.

At home, he's no better off. He's all worked up about his pregame speech, which, at this rate will be more of a mess than I thought was possible. He keeps trying to eat his lip due to the Novocain. Dad feeds him chewing gum, thinking it will "wear off," until Colton nearly swallows his own tongue.

My dad is still at it with the miracle stuff, only now he's changed the title of his "accounts" to, "Out on a Limb." Mom tries to be supportive, but with Colton's problems at hand she can do little more than roll her eyes. And it's strange, the way she's tip-toeing around me, asking how *I'm* feeling when Colton looks like he got into a fight with a hornet's nest.

I hide in my room, working with my powers. Where it used to be curses, I'm finding that if I focus, like, really focus, I can do all sorts of stuff without lifting a finger. Lights out? Easy. Dribble a basketball simply by looking at it? Please. Stop the ceiling fan, make it change direction? Cake.

But the truck in the middle of the street? I can't figure out what happened. Did I really stop a two-ton piece of metal and machine without even knowing it? Before I can research any further, Dad taps at the door and says we're leaving in five minutes. I get to work on one last spell, one that will hopefully save Colton from humiliation.

We load up in the van, Dad with that drum-solo-on-the-steering-wheel energy he gets whenever we do something together as a family. We're not even a sports family, really, but with Colton being the guest of honor we sort of have to go to this game.

The whole town is dressed up for the occasion. Banners strewn over the trestles and bridges. BEAT HILLSDALE! on every storefront. It's a big deal, this game, that much is clear. Personally I'd rather be at home brushing up on my spelling materials, but that will have to wait. Colton has big problems.

As it stands, the guest of honor is drooling on his shirt as he looks over his notes. A few nights ago I'd offered to help with his speech but he told me I'd add a bunch of big words he couldn't pronounce. Now, he can't pronounce C-A-T, and I can't believe he just had three cavities drilled out of his mouth as he's expected to give the team a pep talk. This should be good. Even for him.

The stadium is jam-packed. We have to park across the street, where Dad thinks we can make a "quick getaway." My dad is always thinking about saving a few seconds, leaving early, and getting a jump on things. But tonight he's only talking about how it felt to actually fly.

I catch Mom tighten her jaw, blinking and smiling when he starts in about how all the falls and mishaps over the years prepared him for something amazing. Again, I try to downplay things.

"Um, Dad, I don't think wrecking a golf cart was miracle prep."

"Sure it was, honey."

Mom glances back at Colton. And it's still there, that extra something swimming in her eyes. Concern? Intrigue? It's been there since the Piedmont talk, maybe before, but since the near accident it's only stronger. Almost like she's reading into my thoughts or knows something she's not telling. It's not the regular Mom-stuff, it's more serious, deeper. And it's giving me the chills.

She blinks and it's gone. "Colton, how are you?"

"I'm fwime, Merm."

Well, oh boy. I take a breath as we park. We rush toward the stadium. Sure, I told myself I wouldn't interfere, but he's going to go out there in front of hundreds of people and make an absolute mess out of things. So while Dad talks miracles, I get to work.

A soft tingle, some goosebumps, and I turn and look to the sky. The stars flicker and the crescent moon hangs gracefully in the distance. I recite the spell I threw together in my room earlier, just in case. And sure enough, the case is just. I quietly whisper the spell. It helps that Dad left the van headlights on, and he and Mom have to trot back to the car. Colton, my poor brother, needs me.

There. Nothing great, but it should get him through a pep talk to a bunch of football players.

Mom and Dad hurry back to us. Dad is talking with his hands, and when I see him do a flying motion I know he's still talking about his stupid "accounts."

The crowd is worked up, both sides packed in for the big crosstown rivalry. The Peakland High marching band powers through the fight song. As we're making our way around, Mom and Dad nodding hello, Jada Johnson appears out of nowhere.

"Hi, Abby." She clears her throat. "Colton."

Colton sends her his best scowl. Jada smiles. She's decked out in all black, per usual, with a teal scarf. She gestures to the phone in her hand. "Covering the game. The biggest one of the year, right Colton?"

Colton groans. Because Jada was onto him from day one last year, Zach let her have it, calling her a hack. A small war ensued. It's safe to assume there's no love lost between Jada Johnson and my brother.

She looks at me. "I heard there were more interesting events the other day?"

"Yeah." I ignore my brother's scrunched up face. "It was rather wild," I say with a smile. Mom and Dad wave us down. Colton turns and starts for them without saying goodbye. Rude.

Jada nods. "I'll say. Well, good luck, maybe we can catch up later?"

"Sure."

I rush to catch up with Colton, talking to his back because he refuses to look at me. "Look, I ran into her the other day but you have to trust me. Like last year, did I rat you out? No."

He pretends not to hear me. How mature. Back to last year, Colton thought Jada took me on with the paper only to get the scoop on his secret. But I never said a thing so he has to trust me.

"I'm not going to tell her anything, okay? We were sort of friends. Are sort of friends."

Colton glances back at me then waves me off. I know we'll be talking about this later, but for now he's too worked up about his speech.

Coach Hudson, the head coach of Peakland, greets Colton with a nod.

Speaking of last year, if you want to know the truth, I think Coach Hudson is still a little upset with my brother. After his big game, Colton did the right thing by vowing to stop with the glitter. Only he stayed on the team and didn't tell anyone else. He then proceeded to go out and lay a stinker of a game against a team Peakland was favored to beat. We look back on it and joke about it now, but I don't think Hudson is ready to laugh just yet, as he sets a hand on Colton's shoulder.

"How are ya, Clutts?"

Colton nods. He mumbles something no one can hear over all the noise as Coach waves everyone over.

"Okay boys, bring it in, gather around. This is the kid who got it done against these guys last year. He ran wild, never seen anything like it. Thought he might go straight to the pros, but," he looks to Colton, a pained expression on his face. "Then the very next week... Well, doesn't matter. Anyway, gather up. All yours, Colton."

Dad, finally dropping all the memoir stuff, has his phone out and trained on Colton. Dad's big on leadership, and he's tearing up at the moment because here's Colton, leading the varsity football team into battle. Colton takes a breath. Then...

"All right, mates. Gather 'round, will you. So last year, the grime bucks didn't give us a Buckleys' chance at things, hear?"

Dad's head pops up. Mom gasps, although I detect a smile behind the hand that covers her mouth. Some snickers go around, but it's hard to tell with the crowd. Shoot, I must have botched the spell. I ease myself back, out of harm's way, and manage a quick look around. The football team regards my brother as though he's speaking with an Australian accent, which he is.

Oopsie. Though, on a side note, I've cured his slobbering issue. The numbness is no longer a problem—he's not drooling or talking gibberish. He is, however, talking like a boy with a pet kangaroo. Or something like it, I'm not sure what "grime bucks" are. I look around to see if Jada is catching any of this. She waves from the railing, phone out and aimed at us.

Yikes. Unaware or unperturbed, Colton plows ahead, climbing up on a bench for effect, a bit wobbly as he raises his arms, talking with his hands for emphasis. "So we can't let them pull the wool over your eyes, ya hear?"

With a huff, Coach Hudson steps in. "Now Colton, I know you're big into theater, but let's drop the act and get the team focused."

Coach is still smiling, but his eyes tell a different story. His face is flushed, although it's always red, as he cuts a glance at Dad, who's quit with the phone and is looking around with a *what's going on?* type look on his face.

I hide my smile, giggling into my collar until I catch Mom watching me. She doesn't look angry or upset, but, proud? I shake it off. Because how could she or anyone else know I had something to do with this?

Colton, still on his pedestal, nods to his old coach. "Well crikey, blimey, I'll do it, captain."

The team Coach Hudson has worked with to focus and ready themselves for battle has lost all control by now. Coach Hudson's face ripens to a deeper shade. I slide off, trying to slink off somewhere, when Mom catches my shoulder, a hand on my back. I close my eyes and try to fix things.

Colton's eyes go wide, as though he only now realized he's been talking like he's stepped out of an episode of Bluey. He leaps down from the bench but trips and takes a fall. The team breaks into laughter.

Colton gets to his feet and wipes himself off. "Sorry, mates." He pumps his fist. "All righty, we did it last year, and I think we can do it again. Go out there and give them a ripsnorter of a match, all right. On three..."

The team can hardly fit their helmets around their smiles. Coach steps in. "Okay, Smith, Horsley, go out there for the coin toss. Colt, hang back with me."

As the captains head out to the field, the rest of the team is still chuckling, patting Colton on the back, and telling him how funny he is. Colton takes it in stride, even though I'm feeling lousy about messing this up so badly for him. I only wanted to help. He was drooling!

Coach Hudson doesn't find the humor in the situation. He's basically got smoke coming out of his ears. "You want to tell me what that was all about?"

"I really can't say, coach. I went to the dentist office earlier and had me some work done, then I..."

Coach Hudson waves him off. "Just go find a seat. We'll call you down at halftime. Try and get yourself together," he says, more to Mom and Dad than to Colton.

We hike up the bleachers, Jada watching like a hawk as the parents and fans call out to Colton. Like I said, he's sort of a legend after leading the team to victory against Hillsdale last year, even if he did follow it up with one epically lousy game.

The band cranks up and we settle in for kickoff. Dad bops along, watching intensely because he not so secretly cares more about the marching band than the team, as he used to be a band geek himself.

I lean in close and whisper to Colton. "So, um..."

"What did you do?" he says, still in the accent.

"I was only trying to help."

"Well, bloody good job you did, 'tisn't it?"

Bad as things are, it's impossible not to laugh. And to my disbelief, Colton is laughing, too.

Mom turns to us, that know-all look in her eyes. Colton smiles at her then turns to me with a giggle. Dad breaks his trance with the band and joins in the staring match. "Colton, what was all that about? What's with the 'mate' and the 'shrimp on the barbie?' You know, there's a time to horse around and a time to be serious, and this was—"

"Dad," Colton says, suddenly in his regular voice. "I got it. I'm sorry. I guess it was the numbness wearing off," he says, rubbing his jaw. I look him over, wondering how I did it, when I lock eyes with Mom. She turns back to the game.

Dad frowns, but he pats Colton's shoulder, pleased with my brother's answer. "Okay, okay. Well, as long as you know.

Colton nudges me. "Look, I know you were trying to help, but stop it. Remember you were going to lay low? You're not laying low."

"Sorry. I really didn't mean it. I just..." I catch Mom's eye again and sink low in my seat. "Sorry," I whisper.

Chapter 10

Peakland falls behind quickly. They're down ten points in the first quarter before they rally to tie things up by halftime. Colton gets through his speech, I think, I stay far away where I can't hear if he stumbles and stammers or says something stupid. In the second half, Hillsdale pulls away, and they're up by two touchdowns when Dad, thinking about postgame traffic, decides we all need Michelangelo's Pizza. We "get a jump on things" and make our way down the bleachers, Hillsdale scoring once again before we get to the gates.

We arrive at Michelangelo's around eight. The place is nearly empty, and Heather, the super nice girl at the register, welcomes us and tells us to sit wherever. It's slow, maybe six people there. A man sitting by himself, playing a game on his phone. A couple, smiling at each other, talking about a movie they've just watched. A family of three waits on a to-go order.

Colton is in an especially good mood, laughing about his funny Australian accent. Dad says it reminds him of a piece he read in Reader's Digest about a woman in Alabama who was in a car crash only to wake up from a three-day coma to speak with a British accent for the rest of her life.

We place our order and get our drinks when Mom, who's been mostly quiet since the game, out of the blue clears her throat and says, "So Abby, have you given any more thought to visiting Piedmont?"

Colton turns to me. I cock my head, wondering why she'd pick now of all times to bring that up. "No, actually. I haven't given it a bit of thought."

Dad and Colton exchange looks. Colton raises his eyebrow, probably because of my tone. I've been warned repeatedly about my tone of voice lately, but I can't hide my displeasure with this little ambush.

Mom takes a breath "Well, I just think…"

She's gearing up for a speech when my steaming cheese pizza arrives at our table. Colton always calls me a baby because I don't like a bunch of junk on my pizza, and I'm sure it's what he's getting ready to do when the door to the restaurant opens and three suspicious figures walk in, eyes darting, watching the windows, huddling near the counter. They definitely don't look like parents or fans, with their jacket collars up, hats pulled low, shifting around. They look like they're scoping the place out.

My breath catches. Something is going on. Dad and Colton don't notice, going on about pizza toppings while Mom's back to being quiet and weird. But from my position at the table, through the steam of my hot pizza, I have an unobstructed view of the front. Whatever is happening, isn't good.

At the counter, Heather smiles until the tallest guy leans over close, motioning to the cash register. The hairs on my neck stand to attention as her smile plummets and her eyes go wide. She nods quickly. I'm witnessing something I've only seen in the movies and only a few at that, because Mom is a stickler about the rating system.

It doesn't take a genius to figure out Heather's being robbed, but it's hard to believe. After all, this is East Ridge, where nothing *ever* happens.

Mom clears her throat. She tries again to bring up the stupid Piedmont School. I hear her say something about real life proof that I'm special, but up front, Heather isn't moving fast enough. The lead guy with the scruffy beard grabs her wrist. The other two guys look around, a chunky one with a stocking cap makes eye contact with me. I look to my family, still talking and laughing as Colton plays with his straw. I have to do something.

"Are you okay, sweetie?" Mom reels me in with the question.

I'm not okay.

"Um, I..." I turn to my bathroom excuse again. Colton scoffs, and Mom tells him to cool it, and then they go back and forth. Dad is too busy stuffing his face with a spinach salad.

I start for the restrooms, but once I'm out of sight I crouch and double back along the wall that separates the counter from the dining room. I scurry toward the front, ducking low and getting close enough to hear the tall guy order Heather to get the hundred dollar bills from the floor safe.

Her voice shakes as she tells them she can't. The tall guy starts for her. A dish breaks in the kitchen. Time to act. I step out of the shadows. "Hey. Leave her alone and get out of here while you still can."

The tall guy shoves off the counter and pounces. He looms over me, glancing back to Heather, then over his shoulder to his two buddies. One actually laughs. He turns back to me. "Look, little girl. Go away."

"Yeah, go play with your dolls," says the second one, a short chunky guy with a mole on his chin. He shoos his hands at me. Bad move. Because I'm not in the mood.

I plant my feet and jut my head out. "Last chance to leave and never come back."

This time, even Heather looks at me like I've got crabs crawling out of my ears. Tall Guy makes a show of placing his hands on his hips as he leans down real close, close enough so I can see all the blackheads on his large, bulbous nose. His disgusting smoker breath is hardly neutralized by the spearmint gum he's chewing.

He grits his teeth. "Little girl. Go away."

Tingle city. A wave of chills runs down my back and rolls down my arms. At first I think it's because I'm afraid, because I should be terrified. But I'm not afraid. I'm angry. Because this guy, with his stupid nose, getting in my face, is trying to rob my favorite restaurant. Not cool.

I take a step back and smirk. "Wow, you guys really are a band of idiots."

His eyes widen. "What did you say?"

I shrug. "I mean, a strong-arm robbery at a restaurant, at *dinner*time? Way to think things through—hit a spot during rush hour. Anyone with half a brain cell would come at closing—fewer witnesses and not to mention the till will be full."

The three dunces look at each other. Behind them headlights dance in the parking lot, foot traffic drifts past, horns at the busy intersection in the distance. Still, the tall guy isn't open to my advice. "I've had about enough of your mouth little girl. Run along. We're just here to pay our *bill*," he says with a wink and a chuckle.

Enough is enough. "You want your bill?" I give him my finest sneer. "Fine. You will get a *bill*."

"What in the world does that mean?" Tall Guy stands and snorts. He looks at Heather. Heather's eyes double in size and her mouth drops open. The other two have the same reaction. Tall Guy grits his teeth. "What?"

"Lester, it's, you um. It's..." The chunky guy gestures to his nose. I stand back, arms crossed, hoping this will be enough to end it. And sure enough, when smelly old Lester raises his hand to where his big honker nose used to reside, he finds instead a duck bill.

"What the...?"

He stumbles back with a scream. Forks hit plates. Heather covers her mouth. Two guys from the kitchen rush out, wiping their hands on their aprons before they reach for their phones. "Dude, that's sick!"

We're getting some attention now. Lester looks at me, his eyes wide. "What did you do?"

I tilt my head and smile. "I warned you. That's what I did."

It isn't until Lester goes to reach for something in his pocket that I find it hard to swallow. My blood turns to ice because I'm thinking the worst is about to happen as he fumbles around. Only, when he pulls what used to be his hand out, it's a wing.

Another scream.

"Last chance," I warn. "Or did you want feathers with that order?"

Chunky Guy's gone white as a ghost. "Lester, what in the world happened to your face?"

Lester looks at me, his cold, mean eyes now wobbly with fear. He opens his bill. "*Quack quack quack.*"

With that, all of them begin backing off, feathers fluffing as they shuffle into each other, moving for the door when Sherriff Willoughby walks in.

I'm nearly hyperventilating when the dining area breaks into applause. Customers laugh, and I can only assume they think it's some sort of weird dinner theater thing. By the time they stand, shouting "bravo" all I can do is bow and smile through the fear and adrenaline rushing through my body.

The applause is cut short when Sherriff Willoughby reaches for the cuffs. The show is not over. And just as fast, Lester's face morphs back into his regular ugly mug. His hands, too. Stranger still, is that I'm no longer calling the shots. I'm too overwhelmed.

Luckily, the other two guys are too terrified to do anything other than tremble and stammer, almost like they're *hoping* to go to jail.

Sheriff Willoughby, his face red from exertion, seems otherwise unperturbed. He looks at the other guys. "Man, you three have to be the dumbest bunch of crooks, robbing a restaurant at dinnertime."

Lester looks at me and starts backpedaling. I manage a shrug. The sheriff shakes his head. "Lester, aren't you still on probation? What were you thinking? Come on guys."

Heather wipes her forehead, her hands still shaking as she straightens the cash register where it almost fell off the counter with all the commotion. The cooks and kitchen guys are watching the playback, shaking their heads, asking who caught the best angle as the sheriff herds the three robbers out the door. "Okay, this way. All of you. I'll be back for my order, Heather."

Once the bad guys are escorted out, the restaurant hums with excitement as patrons return to their meals, laughing and shaking their heads at the odd dinner theatrics. But not our table. My family is hurrying over. Great.

My heart rate is nearly normal again when Heather looks at me. "Did you see that? I mean, what in the world? And wow, you were a total bad... I mean, you let those guys have it."

"Oh, no. I mean, I didn't..." I shrug it off as though I have no clue. Which is halfway true, I'll say that much.

She shakes her head. "You know what? This is not worth eight bucks an hour. I can't wait until I leave for school next year."

Dad rushes over. "We thought it was a show."

Heather gushes. "Show? Those creeps tried to rob me. And then..." She takes a breath, probably realizing what it might sound like to say anything else. "And then, I just don't know..."

"Well?" Dad looks at me. "Is everyone okay?"

Heather nods and shuts the drawer to the register. "Sort of, I mean, that was..." She shivers and sets a hand to her chest. She's still too shaken to talk too much. And here comes Colton, followed by Mom, who looks surprisingly calm.

Colton has stars in his eyes, and I think he's walking on his tippy toes. "They were trying to rob you? Like, stick 'em up and stuff?"

"Colton," Dad admonishes. Mom steps forward.

"Well, I'm glad it worked out for the best," she says, looking directly at me. Dad turns to her.

"What's that mean, hon?" He nods to Heather. "This poor girl is probably traumatized, and Abby, I can't believe you just witnessed that."

"I'm okay, Dad."

Heather shrugs it off as well. "Yeah, I'm fine, except, his face." She looks at me, waving a hand over her nose. "I mean, did you see that?"

"Maybe it was the lighting," I say, because Mom is staring at me again.

Heather wrinkles her nose. "No way. That was *not* the lighting."

Colton watches from the window as Sherriff Willoughby calls in the paddy wagon. He's got all three guys on the curb, Lester still holding his face, mumbling gibberish as a line of cars stream into the parking lot. The football crowd is here.

Heather wipes down the counter. "I've had some strange nights in this place, but that takes the cake."

"Yeah," I say, but for different reasons. Because sure, I'm out of control—I tingled and nearly turned him into a duck. But I sure didn't fix him back. Which means if I didn't uncurse him, who did? My jaw drops. I look back at Mom, who quickly looks away.

"Well, we should probably get back to our dinner."

Chapter 11

Sheriff Willoughby returns, and we answer a few questions as he takes down a cannoli the size of his shoe. Mom hands Heather a twenty-dollar tip for her troubles. I'm thinking things might work out when Jada Johnson—who once showed me her police scanner—swings through the door with a ding, huffing for breath. Colton stiff arms her with a "No comment," and we manage to leave before the football team arrives and things really get crazy.

In the car, Dad talks a mile a minute about the strange events taking place in East Ridge lately (his levitation still tops the list). I know I've only added to my list of problems by getting involved back there, but I couldn't just sit back and watch a robbery happen.

Mom stares out the windshield. She's quiet, almost solemn, and I just know Colton is about to tell Dad all about the near wreck at the dentist's office earlier when a WERG News truck races past, hurrying its way to the scene. I slide low in my seat. Great. Just great.

Ugh, so stupid. I mean, a duck bill? How is that not going to grab attention? I need to use my head, be smarter about this. I was flustered, angry, not to mention terrified. Who knows what that Lester guy had in his coat? Was it just a temporary spell? It all happened so fast. I need to practice more, get my temper under control. At least only a few people were there to see it.

At the house, Dad stops and looks up to the tree as he's started to do whenever he gets home. I can't deal, I fake a yawn and tell them I'm beat. Mom nods. Dad's still looking at the tree.

If I thought my brother was going to stay quiet, I was mistaken. Two minutes later comes the loud clomping up the stairs. Colton walks into my room. "Do I even need to say it?"

I plop down on my bed. "I know, I know."

He paces, two steps back and forth. He can never sit still, but when he's worried it becomes unbearable.

At the windowsill he glances down at the quartz stones and quickly backs off. He looks at his hands then wipes them on his pants. "This is getting out of control. The thing with the truck today, the accents, whatever you did back there. What were you doing, anyway? I mean," he shakes his head. "I can't believe what I'm about to ask but, did you turn that dude into a duck?"

I throw my hands down on my lap. "It's, I don't know. It's hard to explain." So many thoughts in my head, swirling, spiraling. It sounds crazy to say, what I'm thinking, but, this is Colton, my brother, and we've been through so much already. I might as well tell him. "But the truck thing? Colton, that wasn't me."

He spins around, his brow scrunched and his cowlick standing at attention. "What do you mean, *it wasn't you*? It was *all* you, sis, and you're doing it so much that you don't even know it. I mean, but thanks again, by the way, you did possibly save Heather's life."

I shake my head. "It doesn't feel that way. It doesn't feel like it was me, not in the truck, or back there, when he... I don't know. It feels like...something's off, Colton." What I can't bring myself to say, is: *I think it was Mom.*

Colton stops pacing and looks down at me. "Look, Abs, you've had a big week, a big day. Saving lives, fighting crimes, but umm, you might want to get things under control, you know?"

Abs? That's a new one. I nod. "Easier said than done."

He picks the cup up off the floor and sets it back on the desk. His face lights up. "So, you've been practicing?"

I can't help my grin. Even though he's the world's biggest goofball, I still, for some reason, cannot help the urge to impress my big brother. I roll my eyes and the cup takes flight. It twirls into the air. It spins and spins, and Colton watches it with complete amazement as I set the cup on his head like a hat.

"I knew it!" He goes from grinning to cocky smirk in a second, swatting the cup from his head. "You know, you sort of have me to thank for all this, Abs. If you hadn't spelled that glitter for me last year you never would have known what you were capable of doing."

"Well, thank you so much," I say with a giggle, because he doesn't notice the cup back in the air, over his head, now full of water. Not before it tilts, and the water comes splashing over him.

"Hey, what in the..."

I shrug. "Stop calling me *Abs*."

Steps thud outside my room, down the hallway. "Hey, you kids all right in here?"

Dad pokes his head in, sees Colton, hair drenched and arms out, dripping water on the carpet. "What in the world?"

"Uh, just an accident, Dad," Colton says, glaring at me.

"Yeah, Colton tripped."

Dad nods, because tripping is a plausible excuse for almost anything when it comes to him or Colton. "Okay, let me get you a towel," he says, looking from Colton to me, to the floor. "Got to be more careful."

When he's gone, Colton looks at me, wiping his forehead.

"You know, Abby, you might want to treat your allies a little better. You're going to need my help."

"Am I?" I shoot him a smirk. He looks ridiculous.

He sticks a finger in his ear. "Yeah, you are. Because you obviously can't control your temper."

"Can too," I blurt, then I stick out my tongue at him. He looks at me, then runs a hand through his wet hair.

"Yeah, okay. Sure you can."

Chapter 12

On Monday, school goes mostly according to schedule. Mr. Wolff makes a grand gesture of his return to power. In his crisp charcoal suit, he nods and greets students at the entrance, offering words of wisdom, doing his best to show he is in perfect health.

I don't see him until it's too late. I attempt to slide by, to blend in and scoot through the herd without being noticed. I'd like to get some study time in with my word lists. No such luck.

The principal calls me over. "Miss Clutts. Abigail Clutts," he says in a way that means *come here right now*.

I stop, like a fish swimming upstream, backtracking over to him. It's not easy, people are rude. They'll shoulder you and never look back. But I can't let myself get worked up about such things, even when Steven Chowder knocks one of my backpacks right off my shoulder and keeps thumping along, the jerk.

Focus. I need to be on my game. I put on my best smile as Mr. Wolff looks me over with that huge, fake, toothy smile of his. "Good morning, Abigail."

"Good morning, Mr. Wolff." I've told him three time that I go by Abby. If someone can't get your name right after three corrections, well, what's the use? Regardless, Mr. Wolff shows no signs of a man halfway turned into a donkey. And he's still just as arrogant as ever.

I wait for him to get to the point. A bell rings, and he motions for the foot traffic to hurry along. He nods to a few teachers, ones who probably already secretly hate his guts. I heard he made them come in on weekends over the summer. That sort of thing can't go over well with the staff.

Eventually, he turns his dark beady eyes to me. "I thought I'd check in with you. I hear you had quite a scare on Friday night. Everything okay?"

Great, he's heard about that. I think back to the news truck rushing to the scene. I'd forgotten to check the news to see what was reported.

"Yes, we're fine. It was, a scare, I mean. But, we're safe now."

I'm rambling because I don't know how to stand or where to put my hands. And my smile, it's way too big. I try to take it down a notch, but I can't help it, this guy throws me off. But why? Why would he suspect me of...hmm, I can't say what. It would be ridiculous for him to think I turned him into a jackass before the entire school, right? I almost laugh thinking about it, until he strokes his chin.

"Well, great. I'm not sure what's going around, but it's something, and I plan on getting to the bottom of it." Another nod, wave, laugh. Then he turns to me in a way that gives me the shivers. "I think it's all related."

Gulp. I look off to the dwindling line of students rushing past, trying not to appear as frazzled as I feel. But a wave of heat rushes to my face. I wipe my forehead. "You do?"

"Oh yes. First with Chaz, then Reagan. And that thing at the assembly. The robbery attempt. As it's being reported, it all seems rather odd, no?"

"Oh, I can't say, I missed it."

He turns and faces me. "But you were there, correct?"

"Well, yes." My voice whines like a vacuum clogged with

dirt too large to pass. The second bell rings. Mr. Wolff tightens his jaw.

"Come along, I'll walk you to class."

I guess I have no choice in the matter. Mr. Wolff turns me for the hallway, where it's quiet and I'm late. I hate being late. And his hand on my shoulder sends a frigid shiver through my back. My body is urging me to run. To get away from him, now.

"Seems you've had a front row seat to all of this strangeness, Miss Clutts."

"Not really, I mean, it all happened so fast," I say, because that's what people say about these things. Mr. Wolff nods.

"So, did you see anything peculiar about the suspects? Anything with their...faces?"

"Well, I don't know. I was only trying to have dinner with my family." And then for no reason, I add. "We thought it was theater."

A gleam shimmers in his eye. "Yes, oh, I'm sure. Colton, your brother, I saw his file. He was into theater, no? And sports, too, no? Ah, it's too bad we can't get him running around again like last year. Sort of a flash in the pan, wasn't it? I also read your file. Shame what happened at last year's spelling bee. But we learn from our mistakes, no?"

Okay, now he's pushing it. I swallow my rebuttal, but with it comes a slight tingle in my scalp, down my neck, only to fizzle out when it gets to where his hand is on my back. He chuckles. "Ah, better luck next time."

We round the corner, and we're almost at Ms. Franklin's class and all I want to do is break away from his clutches, when he turns me to square up and face him. There's a cloud of darkness in his eyes I didn't notice earlier, like a grayish storm in his gaze. I suppose it's been there all along.

My feet freeze in place as his smile drops completely. "I do wish to be clear. I will get to the bottom of this. In fact, I have some theories, ones I'm not at liberty to discuss just yet, but rest assured, I will soon. And when I do—"

"Abby, my Shakespearean. There you are."

Ms. Franklin to the rescue. Mr. Wolff straightens, the toothy grin returns. He chuckles, and I do all I can not to run and hide behind my English teacher.

"Ah, just chatting with Miss Clutts, is all. Sorry I kept her."

Ms. Franklin motions to the classroom. "No problem, everything okay?"

I use this opportunity to break free, but first I catch a glimpse of Mr. Wolff's eyes again. Yikes. He turns his attention to Ms. Franklin. "Oh yes, everything is splendid. In fact, Abigail and I were just discussing how there's an explanation for everything. And I think soon we'll get it."

Ms. Franklin looks back to me, a bemused smile on her face. "Oh, okay, well, class is starting."

Mr. Wolff tips his head and starts down the hall. He flexes his hand, the one that was on my back. "We'll talk later, Abigail."

As I watch him slink off, I shake off the ice and whisper to myself. "It's Abby."

"WHAT DO you mean he knows? That's—*argh, umph* —ridiculous."

I try not to laugh at my scrawny brother struggling with dumbbells he thinks are going to make him buff. He does three curls before a bead of sweat pops out on his forehead. He struggles to do a fourth, only to drop the weights in exhaustion.

What's not funny is the smell. Colton's bedroom reeks of fungus or pork rinds. Like feet. His clothes are all over his floor, and the mumble rap certainly isn't helping things. He picks the weights up and I shrug, wondering what I expected by telling him about the odd encounter with Mr. Wolff.

"I don't know, just that, he knows I've got something to do with it."

"*Argh...* You've got *everything* to do with it."

"Yes, I know. Thank you very much. But he shouldn't know that."

Two more curls and Colton sets the weights down, catches his breath, and checks himself out in the mirror. I'm not sure what he sees, but he looks awfully pleased. I resist the urge to tell him that two days of "weight lifting" isn't going to do much in the way of results, especially considering he's using Mom's little green aerobic weights. But I bite my tongue. As much as I hate to admit it, I need him on my side.

"Abby, let me give you some advice," he says, flexing his arm. He bends down to pick the weights up again. "This is my third year at Peakland Middle, and in those three years I've seen my share of teachers and principals."

I cross my arms. "Is this going anywhere?"

"Look, what I'm trying to say is, Mr. Wolff isn't exactly the most observant guy. I mean, I'm sure Mr. Morton brought him up to speed, you know, about last year, when the glitter fad was going on, when I was running all over everyone and even got promoted to high school football. And he hasn't said a word to me about that, so..." Colton shrugs.

My brother will take any excuse to remind people he played for the Peakland High Panthers for two games, when he had magical glitter thanks to yours truly. Things didn't exactly end well, but that part never quite makes the story.

"That's just it, though. He *did* say something about you."

Colton drops a weight on his foot. "Ow!" He grabs his injured foot, hopping on the other. "Ouch, ouch, ouch."

I roll my eyes and wait him out. Ha, *weight* him out. I'm giggling when he stops hopping around. "What's so funny?"

"Nothing."

He rolls his eyes. "So, what exactly did Wolff say?"

I shrug. "He said he wished you were running around like you did last year, or something to that effect."

Colton stares at me. "And what's *that* supposed to mean?"

"I'm not sure," I say, lifting the weights with my eyes. I send them floating up and down, Colton's eyes light up as he watches in a trance before he snaps out of it and grabs the weights from the air.

"Well, you need to get a grip, sis. If you're not more careful, people are going to find out about you. And if that happens, all the little magic tricks in the world aren't going to save you."

My temper gets the best of me. A flush of hot lava anger builds as I stare Colton down, and then...

"Um, what are you..."

A rush of warmth reaches my face. The frustrations at school, what Mr. Wolff said about the spelling bee. Before I can stop myself I've lifted my brother off the floor. I flip him upside down.

"Abby, what are you..." Colton looks down, which is up, then up, which is down. "Abby, cut it out!"

I cross my arms. Tilt him one way, then the other. "Say you're sorry."

"Uh..." His hair falls to the floor, the weights hit the carpet. "Okay, okay, sorry, I'm sorry. What am I sorry for?"

"*Little* magic tricks? Is that what you think this is?"

I flip him back around and set him safely on his feet. He runs to the bed and plants his butt on the mattress. "What in the... Abby, you gotta get a grip."

Maybe he's right, I do need to get a grip, not that I'll admit it to him. "Look," I point at him. He flinches. Hmm, having this kind of power is gratifying. No more *little* Abby. No more teasing. No more walking all over me. Colton backs away and I laugh.

"I'm under a lot of pressure, okay? I've got Mom looking at me like I'm a space alien and Mr. Wolff watching my every move and the last thing I need is you getting all bossy on me, got it?"

"Yeah, yeah. Sheesh. It's just that..." he takes a breath. "Remember all that stuff you said to me last year? About not showing off? Well, it feels like *you're* kind of showing off this time."

I give it some thought. Am I showing off? Perhaps. But... "Hello, I stopped an armed robbery. I saved *your* life. I'm taking the fight to bullies and making things right for those who can't or won't stand up for themselves."

Colton stands and begins pacing his room. "Okay, fine. But, it seems like this is more about you than saving the world. It's all over your face. You're on a power trip, and I'm a little worried about how this is going to end."

"So what, you're going to go tell *Mommy* and *Daddy* I'm a superhero? That I spun you around the room?"

"No," he says, way too seriously. "But listen to yourself. You're the one calling yourself a superhero. Anyway, I'm not going to do that, okay? You looked out for me when I was Colt the Bolt, so I'll let you figure things out on your own."

I start to thank him when he raises his hand to stop me. "Unless, you get out of hand. If you start flipping cars around the parking lot and turning the school into a Transformers movie, well, I'll have no choice but to run to Mom and Dad. Are we clear?"

I stifle a laugh at him thinking that if I did go on such a rampage, Mom and Dad of all people would be able to stop me. Then again—Mom. I need to find out what's going on with her.

I shake it off. I have no such plans. I'm only going to stop bullies at Peakland Middle. To me at least, that is a noble goal. So I shrug. "Fine. Thanks, bro."

"Yeah, sure. Now can you get out so I can finish lifting?"

"Oh, right. Have fun."

Chapter 13

Tuesday is Dad's night to cook, also the weekly test for our smoke detectors. After school it's just the two of us. Mom is working late and Colton is at practice. Max sits on my feet under the table.

I'm reading Jada's latest story. She's demanding people come forward and stop ignoring all the weird things going on at Peakland Middle School. She even links it all the way to last year's odd occurrences on the football field with uncanny accuracy that makes the hairs on my skin stand to attention. Then she goes into Colton's pregame speech, claiming he was "speaking in tongues." Wow, so much for accuracy. Besides, for a freshman reporter my old mentor is coming off a bit obsessed with her old middle school. Let it go, Jada.

I'm shaking my head as I read over the story while Dad "preps." It's clear he has lofty culinary goals this evening, whistling a tune as he cuts up the chicken he's marinating. He's even wearing his *Mr. Good Lookin' is Cookin'* apron and referring to me as his sous chef.

At least he's dropped the whole floating down from the tree thing for now. It's one of my father's finest qualities—his ability to get sidetracked.

At the counter, he reads from his iPad—which is dinged and cracked and covered in flour. "All right, my dear, we've seasoned with salt and pepper and paprika. Now we shall cook in a large skillet over medium heat." He glances back at me. "I think we can handle that."

I turn away from Jada's stupid story and smile at Dad. Mom tells me not to encourage him, but I can't help myself. I like his spirit.

With that he tosses in the chicken. It sizzles as it hits and he adds olive oil. I pretend I'm not watching closely, which I am. I'm watching super closely.

"All righty, next we shall get the water to a simmer, and..."

He spins off for the sink, unknowingly knocking the handle of the skillet and sending the chicken flying in the air. From my place at the dinner table, I manage to right the skillet, use it to catch the chicken, and place it back on the burner before he even thinks to check on things. I shoot him another smile. My practice has paid off.

None the wiser, Dad fills the pot and brings it over, checking the chicken and looking satisfied. Disaster averted.

Seven disaster diversions later, I'm able to get a minute with Dad to talk about this Piedmont thing.

"Okay sweets, immobilize."

"Immobilize. I-M-M-O-B-I-L-I-Z-E. Immobilize. Hey Dad, I really don't want to start at a new school. I just got comfortable at Peakland."

As much as I hate to do it, I give my voice a bit of extra girly whine. A slight pout seals the deal. Dad looks at me and melts.

"Correct. I think." He removes his Ove glove. "I know, dear, I've spoken to your mom about this. She still wants you to do the tour, but I'm kind of thinking we can work this out."

I get to my feet. Max jumps up and barks. "Really?"

He nods. "Yeah, you're doing so well. Even with all this strangeness. I'll talk to her, okay?"

"Thanks, Dad."

I'm coming in for a hug when Colton and Mom walk

through the door. Colton gives me a *what are you up to* glare. Mom's too busy looking around, bracing herself for disaster.

"Hey guys. How's it going?" she asks, searching for smoke, fire, charred remains of dinner. With nothing out of order she smiles, pleasantly surprised. Meanwhile, Dad's apron is covered in stains. Not much I could do about that.

"Wow, Rob. This is..." Mom looks over the spread. I set the table, four plates, cloth napkins, a vase full of wilted wildflowers I was able to revive. I even light the candles when no one's looking. Not a match in sight.

Nothing makes my mom happier than all four of us sitting down to eat dinner together. "This is so nice." She's beaming, unlike Colton, who levels a glare on me.

I shrug and mouth "What?" I haven't done anything wrong. I mean, keeping Dad from burning the house down while manipulating him to take my side with the whole switching schools thing isn't so bad. Is it?

Colton shakes head. "I'm going to shower."

Dad, nearly knocking over the entire bowl of salad, removes his apron. "Well hurry, dinner is getting cold." He looks at me and winks. The guy is awfully proud of himself. I'm glad I could help.

Ten minutes later we sit for dinner. Colton, his hair still wet from his shower, eyes me like I'm about to combust.

Mom dishes out the chicken pasta entrée, shaking her head, marveling over how Dad pulled it off. She didn't even have to use the fire extinguisher she keeps under the sink.

They start talking about work. Colton avoids my eyes. I guess he's still upset with me for spinning him around upside down in his room the other night. I realize I'm going to have to cool it with the stunts if I'm ever going to get through this. I need my brother on my side, especially with Mr. Wolff watching so closely. I'm thinking about that when Mom sets her fork down with a clank.

"Oh." She hops up so suddenly her chair tips. "I have just the thing to go with this."

Dad frowns as Mom whirls to the counter, where she reaches in the top cabinet and pulls out a lump of tin foil, talking over her shoulder. "I um, made some bread the other day. It's enriched, I mean delicious," she laughs. "Anyway, I want you both to have a piece." She brings it over and unwraps it.

Dad looks at us, then to Mom. "Claire, I have bread. It's the cheese kind we like so much."

Mom shakes her head, like a swarm of bees is flying around her face. "No, this is what they need. I mean, they should try this. Both of them."

Colton, hater of trying new foods, balls his face up. "I think I'll stick with Dad's cheesy bread."

Dad smiles.

"No!"

We all turn to Mom, who recovers with a deranged smile. She walks over to Colton's side of the table and thrusts a slice of bread at his face like she's about to jam it down his throat. "Here, try."

He takes the bread, looking around. Then Mom moves to me, shaking a piece of bread. "You too, Abby. Eat."

It's clear she's not taking no for an answer. I eat the bread, which is a little dry but not too bad. After some threats and prodding, realizing Mom isn't going to stop until we've both eaten the stupid bread, Colton manages to eat his too.

Dad smiles. "Well, okay, if we're all eating this..." He reaches for the bread but Mom swats his hand away.

"No, no." She recovers with a laugh. "It's uh, it's just for the kids."

Dad takes it in stride. Appeased, Mom clears her throat, resuming the dinnertime discussion. "So Colton. Abby. I assume it was an uneventful day at Peakland Middle School? At least in comparison to recent days. I didn't get any text alerts, so I take it that's a good sign."

I chew on my dinner. Honestly, my dad's chicken is a bit gamey for my taste, not that I would ever tell him that. We've suffered so many Tuesday night mishaps, as Mom and I call them, that we're just happy nothing is ruined, broken, stained, or burning.

"Um, nope. Nothing much going on," I manage. It's the truth though. In fact, this week, besides the run in with Mr. Wolff, things have been rather normal. But then I think about how I played Dad during dinner, and I'm hit with a twinge of guilt. Still, I hope he'll come to my rescue when or if Mom brings up the Piedmont thing, although she hasn't said much of anything lately. I'm sort of hoping it's all forgotten.

Colton slams down his glass of milk and lets out a disgusting burp. "Yeah, nobody turned green today, so there's that."

Mom asks my brother to mind his manners while Dad whips his phone out and snaps a picture of his plate. He fiddles with the phone until he sees Mom's face and then says "sorry" and pockets the phone. He places his napkin on his lap.

"Well, that's great," he says, still marveling over his dinner success.

Mom nods. "It *is* great. Maybe things can get back to normal around here for a change."

Colton snorts and glances at me. "Yeah, wouldn't that be something."

I know I should leave it be, but I can't stand the dread that's been sitting in my chest since Mom brought up this private school thing. I know if I don't say something now I'll toss and turn all night and end up grumpy at school, and that won't be good for anyone. I shoot Mom my finest pout. "Um, on that note, I was thinking. I really don't want to go to a new school."

I'm expecting a fight. And Dad does too, judging by how quickly he looks up from his plate. Colton looks the way he always looks: confused.

Mom nods, sips, and then says, "I know dear. It's why we didn't go to the tour."

"Huh? What do you mean?"

Her mouth is drawn, her shoulders sag. She looks so disappointed. And while I should be happy or relieved, I'm not. My stomach drops. Mom forces a smile.

"It was today. I canceled. I figured you're right, you're doing so well at Peakland, it wouldn't be right to tear you away from your friends."

Friends. As in two. Chucky. Ahmad. Everyone at the table knows I don't have a long list of friends. Dad smiles and says something about how cooking chicken is all temperature and timing. And I should be smiling, relieved, happy I'm off the hook, but I'm not. I only want to know more about Mom. About this Piedmont School that doesn't exist.

In my room after dinner, I'm flying the cup around when I should be doing word study, or debate prep, online chess, or anything to get my mind off dinner. But I also need to work on my control and my temper and why I feel so bad about this whole Piedmont thing. I got my wish, and I should feel grateful, but the disappointment in Mom's face sticks with me.

What's the use? I set the cup down and try to focus on my spelling words when there's a knock at the front door.

Max goes crazy, flying to the living room with his ears up and his fur ruffled. Heavy footsteps clomp downstairs. Dad tells Max to pipe down. I edge out from my room to see what's going on.

Sheriff Willoughby? What's he doing here? He tips his hat,

something I've only seen on one of Dad's old-timey sitcoms. "Evening, Rob."

"Hi, Sheriff," Dad says politely but with an edge that means, *what in the world are you doing here at eight o'clock at night?*

The sheriff hems and haws until Dad invites him in. Max settles into a low growl instead of barking. Mom walks in and asks if she can get the sheriff anything. The sheriff, who has no idea how to cut to the chase, smiles and shuffles his feet.

"No thank you, ma'am. I was just in the neighborhood, had a few questions about the other night, at the restaurant. That is, if you don't mind?"

Dad shakes his head. "Uh, yeah, sure. No problem."

No problem? How about big problem. I mean, hello, you have the suspects. What are you doing here?

"So um, I figured I'd cover my bases, is all. We still have Lester Mayes at the station. He's talking crazy, though," Willoughby says with another round of chuckles. "It's the darndest thing. He says, um, I'm not sure how to put this." I ease down the steps as the sheriff lowers his voice. "He says Abby did some magic."

Another laugh, this time from Dad. Every hair on my neck stands to attention. This is no good. This is no good at all. This is horrifying. H-O-R-R-I-F-Y-I-N-G. I take deep, quiet breaths, trying and failing to slow my racing heart, even as Dad scoffs. "Well, um, that's interesting for sure. Magic, huh?"

For a split second I just know Dad will put it together. Out in the yard, floating down from the limb. *Abby did some magic.* Luckily, Sheriff Willoughby waves it off. "I know, I know."

The sheriff glances toward the kitchen, more likely searching for cupcakes or donuts than a suspect—in this case, me. It's no secret our sheriff loves dessert, and as he adjusts his belt, his belly spilling over the buckle, it's clear he can't say no. "He says she cast a spell on him. Now, I'm not in the business of believing much of anything Lester Mayes says, but I'll say this: that rascal is either the finest actor or he's lost his marbles. He's refusing to eat, won't come out of his cell, and he's got a case of the shakes like you ain't never seen."

Mom steps in with a little muscle in her voice. "And you're doing what, exactly, by coming here, *investigating?*"

Sheriff Willoughby laughs. "Oh, no, ma'am, it's loony, I know that. As I said, I was in the neighborhood and..."

Mom shifts. "And?"

"Well, I uh..."

"Yes?"

"Well, just thought you needed a good laugh, is all." Another peek to the kitchen. "That your little girl has a well-oiled criminal sitting in his cell, crying for his momma," he says with a chuckle.

Dad laughs but Mom doesn't even smile—a clear signal this little meeting is over. Even Willoughby gets the hint. Another tip of the hat. "Well, sorry to bother you folks so late."

Mom only nods. The sheriff turns for the door. "You know, the one thing that gets me about all this—and again, I know it's just Lester being Lester—but..."

"But?" Wow, Mom's patience is shot.

"Well, when I first walked in...this sounds crazy, but...ah never mind. But we did uh, we found uh, these feathers in his pants, in his pockets and at the scene. It's just, we sent 'em to a lab for testing, but it's certainly odd, that's all."

My throat closes up. *The scene?* A lab? If this was nothing why are the feathers going to a lab?

Mom says something I can't understand. And with that, Dad walks the sheriff out to his cruiser. I creep back up the stairs where I dash to the window and watch them out in the driveway. Dad, being his normal, aww shucks self, and the sheriff shaking his head, telling him he meant no harm by coming out. Tell the missus I'm sorry and all.

My head spins. My chest flutters. So, why did the sheriff stop by? Does he suspect me? Does he really think I spelled Lester Mayes? He couldn't. But the feathers. I was about to turn Lester Mayes into a real live duck, and now they've got the feathers to prove it. In a lab!

Soon I'm pacing my room like Colton. I grab the cup and stuff it in the trash can, promising myself right then and there I'm through with spells and magic and witch stuff for good. Forever and ever. I can't risk getting caught. I've read about the Salem trials. Nope, not happening.

I, Abby Clutts, am through once and for all with being a witch.

Chapter 14

Whatever Dad says to Sheriff Willoughby works. I'm not questioned or arrested or thrown in jail. But walking to school the next morning, my brother is uncharacteristically silent, which tells me all I need to know.

It's just the two of us because Zach has overslept again. Fine with me, I sort of need some brother-sister talk time. Skipping along the sidewalk, I try to convince Colton, as much as myself, that all is good. Sort of.

"Look, I know what you're thinking. But Sheriff Willoughby doesn't suspect me. Honestly, how would that sound? I can see it now, Willoughby running to the courts, 'Quick, I need a warrant. Abby Clutts is turning people into ducks.'"

Ten steps later, when I'm about to scream, Colton turns to me. "Okay, I'm only going to say this once. I don't think Sheriff Willoughby suspects you of turning Lester Mayes into a duck."

That does the trick. Soon I'm giggling, my feet lighter and sliding off the curb onto the street. Colton snorts like a pig and that gets us both cracking up. And for the next few steps, everything is like it was before the middle school. Before the spells. Fun.

But it's short-lived. As we get to the parking lot, he turns to me. "Just promise me you'll try, Abby. Try not to make any trouble today, okay?"

I shake my head. "You know, I never thought I'd see the day that *you* were telling *me* not to get in trouble."

"Yeah, well, that day is today." Colton straightens. I turn to find Zach shuffling up behind us.

"Hey guys, sorry I'm late." He stops, folding over, catching his breath. "What's up, a Clutts family pep talk?"

Colton's eyes flick to me. "Something like that."

"Hey Abby," Zach says, his eyebrows doing pull ups with his smile.

"Hey Zach," I mumble.

Ugh. For a few hours one time long ago I might have had the teensiest crush on my brother's best friend. And so when I was doing spells on the glitter, I sort of made one for him too and he enjoyed a brief stint as a world class gymnast/cheerleader. Then I came to my senses and un-spelled it mid-game. Poor Zach went falling flat on his face. And yet, he still looks at me like he thinks I think he's a superstar.

He fixes his hair and grins. I turn my head because it's too much to bear.

"So, you guys talking about the story? Seems like old Jada is at it again."

Colton and I both whirl around to him. Colton says, "What story?" and I say, "Another story?" in unison.

Zach steps back. "Seriously? Don't you guys do current events? Anyway, lead story in *The Peakland High Times*. Lester Mayes is claiming he was hypnotized. He's saying—get this—he was turned into a duck. That's why he was robbing the restaurant. Can you believe this guy? I mean, I've heard of some crackpot defenses, but the old got-turned-into-a-duck defense? New to me. Hey, what's with you two?"

I realize my mouth is wide open. Colton's too. He snaps out of it first. "Huh? Oh," he laughs. "Just, wow. That is insane."

I nod like crazy. "Um, yeah, sounds wacky. I mean, he was

going to rob Michelangelo's from the start, not *because* he was a duck. How lame. Ha, get it, *Lame* Duck?"

Colton covers his face. "Abby, not now. And I warned you about Jada."

Zach shakes his head. "Yeah, um, I thought the whole *turned into a duck* was the weird part, but okay."

Zach looks from Colton to me, eyebrow cocked. "Speaking of weird, what's up with you two?" He leans closer, lowering his voice, gesturing grabby hands. "Okay, spill it. What's going on?"

Colton squirms, and I know I'm roadkill then because he keeps nothing from Zach. He told him everything last year, and Zach went on a promotional campaign for my brother, so I'm not so sure I want Colton to spill it here.

"Noth*ing*," I say. "Nothing at *all*." I aim this warning at Colton, but Zach gives him the you'll-tell-me-later look and it's all I can take. I start for the entrance before I turn Zach's ears into wings and have them carry him away.

The last thing I hear behind my back is Zach's squeaky voice. "Dude. Did Abby turn Lester Mayes into a duck?"

THE WAY I SEE IT, Jada was only reporting a story that makes Lester sound like a loon. I set it out of mind and get through first period without incident. No spells, no problems.

Then I get to social studies.

I'll admit it. Social studies is a subject I give little thought to because I'm usually doing equations in my head, but when Mr. Dabney hands back our pop quizzes from last week, I gasp in horror.

Mr. Dabney jerks to stop. "Abby? Are you feeling okay?"

Okay? Not even close. My quiz has a big fat B on it. I don't get *B*'s. It's obscene, so loopy and weird that it steals my breath.

A film of sweat covers my forehead. My tongue goes dry and scratchy, like it's been dragged along a brick building. I look up to Mr. Dabney and find a small smile lurking beneath the goofy hipster mustache he's growing out. He thinks he's cool. He's not.

"I, this..." I search the answers. The short pop quiz was on the Tariff Crisis during the Jacksonian era. There's been a lot going on, but still, a *B*? How?

Mr. Dabney turns away, performing for the class. "Oh, Abby, I wouldn't get too worked up over missing a single question. You could always reread the chapter."

The class chuckles. Everyone but Ahmad. I turn around and he gives me a look like, *let it go*. But I can't let it go. And I don't find the humor in Mr. Dabney's joke. And besides, looking it over, I'm not so sure I've missed anything.

"Um, Mr. Dabney?"

He spins around, not so playful now. I hold the paper up. "It says here that I got question six wrong, but clearly the house passed the compromise tar—"

He holds up a hand. "Abby, please. This is not the time to argue over a question about the quiz. You can meet me after class if you'd like and we..."

"I wasn't arguing."

"Well, now you are," he says, and the class chuckles again. *Grr.* I hate how he always plays to the class like it's his own personal comedy show. Only, he's not funny, and now the tingles are crashing down as I look at that stupid mustache on his face. After class he'll sit back, finger combing it as he tells me to ease up, it's only a quiz. Only, I've never gotten a B before so it's not all that easy to deal with.

My breath is shaky, my fingers tremble. Mr. Dabney, the worm, is trying to wriggle his way out of admitting he was wrong. And he's embarrassing me—E-M-B-A-R-R-A-S-S!—with his little showman's waltz around the classroom, talking about how pop quizzes are merely a gauge to see where we stand, and we certainly shouldn't get all worked up about it, and...

Someone two rows over raises her hand.

"Yes, Desiree?"

"Um, Mr. D, you have something on your..." Desiree motions to her upper lip. Mr. Dabney stops, wiggles his nose. He stumbles back, and now it's his turn to gasp as he finds that yes, he does in fact have a real live slug on his upper lip where his stupid mustache used to sit.

Who's laughing now? Not Mr. Dabney. Another shriek as he tosses the rest of the quizzes in the air, jumping up and down as the class erupts into chaos. Papers go flying and chairs fall sideways as everyone jumps out of their desks, while others knock into everything in their path as they bolt out of the room.

I sit quietly at my desk, arms crossed as the room clears. Ahmad lingers for a moment before ducking out to the hallway. And then it's just the two of us, as Mr. Dabney falls into a corner, moving his lips, swiping at his mouth, trying to fling the giant, gray, slimy slug from his face. I know I should stop, but I can't help myself.

"Argh," Mr. Dabney curls up, still touching at his face. I really, *really* need to put an end to this but the tingles are still rolling over me as I stare at my quiz paper on the floor with all the debris of our classroom. But at least he will listen now.

"All I was saying," I start again, sliding out of my seat and scooping up my paper, scarred and tainted with that infuriating "B." I hear Greenie out in the hall, restoring order, while in the classroom Mr. Dabney fidgets, hands trembling as he tries to rid himself of the slug stuck to his lip. "Is that it was clear these tariffs were not going to be implemented."

"Please!"

He shields himself with his hands. And I must say, what I've managed to set on his lip is some gnarly handiwork, grotesque even. It's like something from a movie. Still, to my point, I shake my paper at him. He flinches, whimpers, then cowers further into his corner. I point to the question. "But do you see? My only contention is that—"

"That will be enough, Miss Clutts."

I turn to find Mr. Wolff looming in the doorway. Quick as I can I glance back to Mr. Dabney, squinting ever so discreetly to let him know I'm not through with him, before I turn the slug back to hair. Honestly, I'm not sure which is more repulsive.

Mr. Wolff approaches the cowering teacher and offers a hand to help him up. "Mr. Dabney, allow me to offer advice. Never let the classroom stampede you in such a way. Once you've lost control, well, it's nearly impossible to gain it back. Now, what, exactly, is all the fuss about?"

I stand before the classroom, the lone student among the wreckage. I'm still clutching that awful quiz in my hand as Mr. Dabney grunts and wheezes, his hands combing around his face. He reminds me of a blind man who's been given the gift of sight.

"It was, I..." My poor teacher is at a loss. But really, what can he say? He can't prove I gave him a slugstache, now can he? No, he can only stammer and stutter, groveling around like a fool.

I'm a bit unnerved by Mr. Wolff's sudden appearance and what he might have seen, but with the matter settled, I turn for my desk to collect my things, when the principal calls for me.

"Abigail. What a surprise. You always seem to be...involved, whenever something peculiar transpires." His gaze falls to my quiz, then back to me. He cocks his head for a response.

Shoot. I clear my throat. "Well, I was hardly 'involved,' as you say. We had a visitor in the classroom. A slug or a worm. Whatever the case, it scared everyone from their places. Mr. Dabney fended it off, though. He was quite brave, I should add."

I do my best to conceal my smirk as Mr. Wolff regards me closely, as though pressing into my thoughts. A teacher peeks in from the hallway to ask about the commotion. From what I can see of the hallway, the class is being held back against the lockers by Greenie, who's going to town with this thermometer gun.

Mr. Dabney, now back on his feet, takes a few deep breaths, perhaps relieved not to have mucous spread on his upper lip. He rushes to his desk, finds a mirror in the drawer, and examines his mustache closely, as though counting each strand of hair. Finally, he shuts the drawer, and only then seems to notice we're in the room and his students are not.

"Well, I just...it was...I..."

As I guessed, he quickly realizes he can't come out and say what really happened. And so he looks at me, then to his desk. "I think the situation has been remedied."

Mr. Wolff turns back to me, his hands clasped behind his back. He bends slightly as he takes me in. "I see. But again, another strange occurrence in your presence, Abigail. How many is that now?"

"It's Abby," I say, my jaw jutting out in defiance.

"Very well. I suppose we should corral your students, Mr. Dabney?"

Mr. Dabney, still touching his face, snaps to and fixes his ruffled shirt. "Right."

He follows the principal out. At the door, Mr. Wolff looks back to me and I give him my best schoolgirl smile. When he's gone, I set my paper on Mr. Wolff's desk.

I look at the B on my quiz and laugh. As if. I'm guessing he'll correct his mistake now.

Chapter 15

Ugh. I have no appetite and don't wish to be around company. At lunch I drop by Mrs. Godfrey's classroom to explain my recent debate prep absences. She understands but hopes to have me back for regionals. Truth is, I love debate, but between chess and spelling and well, my recent activities, I can no longer trust myself to go head to head with anyone. I mean, at this rate, one minute I'll be stating the perks of electric cars and the next my foe will have antlers coming out of his or her head.

I take refuge at the library, where I can think more clearly. I'm beginning to fear I can't control myself. Because bullies are everywhere, and I refuse to let people walk all over me or anyone else simply because they're bigger or considered prettier or more popular. No. Simply thinking about it sets me off, a slight tingle. The floor-to-ceiling curtains wiggle with my thoughts. For too long the bullies have had their way of things. It's time someone stood up to them.

But if this is going to work, I need a new approach. I need restraint. I rub my temples then pull up a copy of *The Peakland High Times* on my phone. To my horror, Zach was right. Where the last story was full of outrageous suggestions and half-truths, this one is accompanied by a picture from the restaurant. And it's clearly Lester and his gang at the register. I stifle a gasp. There's me (am I really that short?), arms crossed, glaring at all four of them, not exactly looking like a scared little girl. But that's not the half of it.

The photo has been enlarged and enhanced, showing Lester in the center with a duck bill on his face. Again, it's a cell phone shot so it's not exactly clear, but what is unmistakable is the shock in his eyes.

Not only that, the account goes into detail, even an interview with Sheriff Willoughby who confirms yes, they have sent "evidence" to the lab.

Evidence. I guess it sounds better than duck feathers.

I take a quick look around, to the heads down at desks, napping, studying, going about with normal lives as my heartbeat thrums in my ears. My only hope is that people will assume he was wearing a mask—a disguise. After all, wouldn't a robber wear something to cover his identity? Sure he would. And who would believe anything else? I picture the headline: MIDDLE SCHOOLER CASTS DUCK BILL SPELL ON WOULD BE ROBBER.

I snort before I can stop myself. A few heads pop up. Laughing to yourself is no way to stay under the radar. I pocket my phone and gather my things.

The good news is that Reagan Roebuck has fully recovered. Her pretty face is once again unblemished and perfect. As I pass her in the hallway, she's taking things well, soaking up the attention and chatting with friends. Like Chaz, she's playing up the victim aspect of things, wiping her hair back, her topaz bluish eyes wide with drama as she recounts her "experience." I groan as I hear the words "skin cream" and "lawsuit" and "cafeteria food." Sheesh, some people just can't take it on the chin. Ha, get it? On the *chin?*

I'm busy cracking up over my own joke when I spot Colton, and he doesn't look happy. Behind him, Zach looks me over, more intrigued than angry, unlike my brother who is basically growling at me.

"Outside, now."

"I'd love to, but I have something..."

He points to the gym. "Now."

"Fine." I turn, keeping an eye out for Greenie as I follow Colton through the gym and outside to the patio. The doors click shut, and from our place on the hill, we have a clear view of the football field where my brother did all those spectacular things last year.

Around the field, kids walk the track. I spot Ahmad in his baggy gym clothes, Chucky struggling to keep in stride. I'm about to wave to them but then Chaz is out there too, laughing it up with a group of boys who all have identical haircuts. He kicks Chucky's heel, making him high step. My pulse spikes. *Grr.* Can't this guy learn a lesson?

"What's it going to take, Abby?"

I shake off my irritation. Colton taps his foot while Zach stands nearby, munching on a granola bar, half of it crumbling and spilling to his feet. The wind picks up, knocking the chain against the flagpole, tossing my hair around. Colton persists. "People are talking. What in the world did you do to Mr. Dabney, anyway?"

He doesn't seem to care about Zach being around, and he doesn't wait for me to answer. "Fine, you don't want to talk? Well then, let me tell you what we've heard already, Abs. Mr. Dabney has left school due to a 'medical emergency.'"

I cut my eyes at my brother, wishing I hadn't. I'm a horrible liar and even worse at hiding my emotions. My face betrays me and Colton knows it. He nods. "That's right. Some sort of issue with his mustache this morning?" He glances at Zach. "You ever heard of such a thing, Zach?"

Munch. Munch. Munch. "Nope."

"Me neither. And Zach, tell me again, who has Mr. Dabney for first period?"

More munching. Zach wipes his face with his sleeve, then nods along. "Abby does."

"Hmm. Why yes, Abby does, doesn't she?" Colton holds a finger to his chin. "Hey Zach, don't you find it sort of odd, a coinky-dink of sorts, that wherever Abby seems to be lately, something weird or strange happens?"

I cock my head. "Coinky-dink?"

Colton ignores me. "I heard Mr. Dabney had worms coming out of his nose. Then Bentley said it was a tumor." He uses his fingers to count. "I've also heard it was mayonnaise, a snake, a huge booger, and—"

"It was a slug!" I blurt out, losing all control. "A slugstache. And he wore it well." I giggle into hiccups, and from there I'm holding my stomach, hardly able to keep from falling over with my laughter. I don't know what it is, but suddenly it's the funniest thing in the world. Just not to my brother.

"Abby."

"Oh, boy. You should have seen his face. He was on the floor, and he..."

"Abby."

I stop laughing, about to ask what he wants from me when Zach steps forward and points to the track. "Uh oh."

Uh oh is right. The three of us turn our attention to the track as Chaz comes sneaking up behind Ahmad. I already know he's about to pants him. Chaz and his creeps think it's funny to run up behind an unsuspecting victim and yank their pants down. Ugh. Unbelievable. The guy is truly unbelievable. What do I have to do to teach him a lesson? Before the thought can process it's washed away by the tingles.

Zach and Colton turn to me as I plant my feet. Colton says something, but I can't hear him. I'm too focused on Chaz, who crouches, arms out, about to pull down Ahmad's pants when instead he goes rolling head over heels. His shoes go flying off his feet, his gym shorts twist up and over where they somehow end up stuck on his head. Oh, and his socks find their way into his mouth.

Zach laughs, spraying granola far and wide. Colton yells at me. "Abby!"

And there lies a jerk, on the track, tangled in his own shorts, his tighty-whities exposed for all the girls to see. They point and giggle while his friends laugh at him. Ahmad turns around and covers his mouth as Chaz, flat on his back, fights to rip the shorts from his head and spit the sock from his mouth.

Cling goes the chain on the flagpole. The wind is gusting now as the coach whistles for everyone to stop "horsing around" and "bring it in."

"Oh, man!" Zach shakes his head. I look at my brother, then to the track where Chaz fights to get his gym shorts off his head. Not gonna happen.

Colton shakes his head, urging me to stop. "Abby quit it. You can't change fate."

I throw my hands up and nod to the track, shouting into the wind as my hair flies over my face. "Sure I can. Haven't you been watching?"

"I mean, what happens when someone gets seriously hurt?"

"Look." I shrug, grab my book bags. I start to storm off when I catch Chucky watching me from the track. He doesn't wave or nod. Only stares.

I turn for the door, talking over my shoulder to Colton. "If Chaz hadn't messed with my friend, none of this would have happened. I'm only helping fate along, giving it a nudge in the right direction."

I go to make a dramatic exit but when I yank on the door to the gym it doesn't budge. I turn back to the track and sigh.

Zap. Chaz gets his shorts off his head, and the filthy sock rolls out of his mouth. He hurries to shimmy them back on. He might be crying, it's hard to tell from here. I throw my hands up.

"Happy now?"

Colton doesn't answer me. I pretend not to see my best friend standing down there staring at me like he knows I had something to do with Chaz's mishap. Colton shakes his head.

Another yank on the door. "Ugh." I stomp my foot and the big metal handle snaps in two and falls to the ground. The door swings open. There, much better.

And with that, I make my dramatic exit.

THE DAY, the week, it's all a bust. It might be nice to get through school without incident. Or maybe not, who knows anymore? I've already lost my temper twice and it's only lunch. I still have three classes to go, and I'd like to get some spelling bee prep done.

But I'm falling apart.

I sling my bags over my shoulders and march forward, ready to climb this mountain of a day. Only there's Mr. Wolff, waiting outside the door to my algebra class.

"Ah, Abigail, just the person I wanted to see."

My shoulders drop. My bags fall. Oh great. "It's Abby."

"Yes, well..." He pushes off the wall. The bell rings and it occurs to me I haven't made it to a single class on time today. My principal doesn't look concerned. "There was an incident on the track a few minutes ago. I hear you and your brother were up on the hill?"

Seriously? Does this guy have spies? Was Greenie up on the roof again? I take a breath to steady my nerves. "Yeah, something like that." I nod toward the classroom. "I really need to get to class."

He sets a finger to his chin. "Your records show you've always been an excellent pupil. In fact, I spoke to Mr. Dabney again. He said you had an issue with an answer on the quiz? That you were awfully worked up about it."

I shrug, realizing he still has nothing on me. Nothing that can stick, anyway. And if this guy doesn't get off my tail, he may grow one. The hall empties, leaving the two of us alone. Again.

I rub a spot in the floor with my foot. "Um, yeah, he made a mistake and marked a question wrong that was clearly correct. That was it. He told me to stay after class, which is why I was there when you came in. And about the track, I assume you're aware Chaz Snead was trying to assault a classmate?"

Mr. Wolff smiles. "I certainly wouldn't say 'assault,' Abigail. But yes, Chaz took quite a tumble, scratched his forehead." Mr. Wolff touches a spot on his forehead, just above the eerie white spot in his brow. Something in his eyes darkens, and I have to look away. The guy really gives me the creeps.

"Did you hear what I said, Abigail?"

"I did. But perhaps Chaz shouldn't have tried to pull down Ahmad's pants, maybe?"

He nods as though convinced of something. "So you were watching rather closely, it appears?"

I shrug. Clearly, it's time for a new tactic. In my best little girl voice, I say, "Mr. Wolff, if it's all right with you, I'd really like to get to class."

"Of course," he replies, ushering the way. "There is, one other thing." He takes my shoulder and steers me to the door of the classroom as though I wouldn't be able to find it on my own. "The door, to the gym. The handle was completely sheared off. Took quite a bit of force—the handle was heavy duty, stainless steel. Do you know anything about that?"

I turn and look up to him. To his dark eyes that swallow me up like the black of the forest. Again, my face must say it all. But he can't possibly think I broke the door, right?

"Yes. Well, I suppose we'll talk later."

With that I turn away, to class, where formulas and equations make far more sense than all the variables going on with Mr. Wolff and this school.

Chapter 23

I skip Spell Club, claiming I need to study for a big test. This raises some eyebrows, mainly Miss Tipton's because everyone knows how badly I want redemption. But I need to get home where I'm safe. Or, where others are safe from me.

Still, my stomach sinks with the weight of the lie, and on the way out, into a light rain, I nearly turn around a hundred times. But alas, I'm burdened with this newfound power, and with that power comes great sacrifice.

Or something like that.

I'm not quite out the door when a familiar voice calls out. "Abby, wait."

I turn around to find Chucky. My sunken stomach now rolling like pizza dough as I remember how he looked up at me from the track. "Hi, Chuck."

He glances back to the classroom. "Hey, I just... I haven't seen you around lately. I mean, earlier, but..."

If I thought it was hard to lie to my teacher, lying to Chucky is ten times worse. I wipe my hair back, staring at my feet. "Yeah, sorry. I've been really busy lately."

"Okay, it's just...things must be hard right now, after that whole thing at Michelangelo's. I'm really glad you're okay."

It's as many words as I've ever heard from my friend, not counting his father's conspiracy theories, which soon follow.

"My dad thinks it's all related—everything. He said

someone posted on a forum about warlock spells. That each of these things follow..."

No. I just can't. "Chucky. I really need to go, okay?"

Chucky's gaze falls to the floor. "Yeah, okay."

I must be the worst friend in the world. Here he's opening up to me, and I'm blowing him off. But I can't talk about this, not now. With a breath, I start off for the exit when he calls out. "I told my dad it would be cool, if it were true."

I stop cold and turn to face him. He looks away and shrugs. "I mean, right? To know someone like that is out there, fighting for us."

Luckily I'm fifty feet away, so hopefully he can't see how my eyes are welling up, how much I want to tell him that I'll fight for him any day. Instead, I give him my best smile. "Yeah, it would. See ya, Chucky."

Colton's football practice has been canceled due to the torrential downpours in the forecast. With Zach in tow, we walk home together, which would be nice if Colton weren't badgering me, asking if I'm happy with all the trouble I've caused.

The wind nearly knocks me back and the sky is a silvery sort of gray. A few drops of rain hit my arms. Colton's all worked up about the track thing. The Mr. Dabney thing. The...everything. I mostly tune him out, until he asks if I have any idea as to why a news truck is parked outside the house. I look up, then hang my head.

Zach starts fixing his hair. "Dude, it's WERG!"

Again, we're no strangers to local stardom. Last year when my brother became an overnight celebrity, Zach became his official PR guy—or more like carnival barker. He started a Twitter trend, did interviews, and made sure Colton stayed far away from Jada Johnson, who quickly connected things with Colton and the magic glitter. Now, watching Zach dash up the steps to our house, where a reporter and cameraman have set up shop, I can already see he's ready to do the same for me.

Only, I have other plans.

The reporter, Blythe Woods, is a complete hack. And so I'm already agitated as we approach the porch where she's talking with Dad. It takes a lot to get my dad worked up, but he sure doesn't look too happy about things, pointing toward the news truck. He sees us coming and moves for the stairs.

"Well, here you are," he says. "Now, Abby, sorry about this, it seems people think they can barge up the stairs with questions about the robbery the other night. Now, if you're not comfortable with any of this, say so, okay?"

I only glare at Blythe Woods. She smiles and fixes her hair. "Hi, Abby Clutts? We just have a few questions..."

The tingles hit without warning. I need to get away, and fast. "I don't feel so well, Dad."

Colton stands at the bottom of the steps, completely ignored by the reporter. Again, this is not WERG's first trip to our house. Last year Blythe came to the house to interview him, only to stab him in the back on the air when everything went awry.

Zach waltzes right up to her. "Hey Blythe, how ya been?"

She politely blows him off, still looking at me. "You are the girl from the restaurant, correct?"

I nod. Dad steps in. "As I've said, I don't think it's a good idea. It was a traumatic experience for our daughter. Now, I'm kindly asking you to leave, or I will call the sheriff."

Blythe nods. "Sheriff Willoughby? Yes, we interviewed him earlier." She turns to me again. "Boy did he have an interesting take on things. But you, Abby, right there in the middle of it all. Were you terrified? Worried about being kidnapped? And about the suspect," she smiles, leaning down to my eyes, all conspiratorial now. "Was it a mask, a duck mask of some sort?"

Zach shoots her a look like she's crazy. "What else could it have been?"

Blythe is still ignoring him when Dad pulls out his phone to make the call, I assume. But it's too late for that, she's already goaded me in. Besides, I have some questions for her. I set a hand on my hip. "Tell me, Blythe, that story you did on those protesters, about the recycling center? Did you guys ever do the follow up, to correct all those false allegations?"

Colton kicks at something on the ground. He grits his teeth and whispers, "Abby, stop!"

I will do no such thing. Not after the last few days I've had. Not with Mr. Wolff hounding me and Mr. Dabney getting on my case in front of the class. Chaz can't seem to stop being a jerk, and that sorry excuse for a sheriff keeps sticking his nose where it doesn't belong. Now the news shows up, staking out my porch, wanting me to talk about a robbery? Ha, no. I don't think so.

Blythe blinks rapidly, flashing her whitened teeth. The town loves her, thinks she's so down to earth. She was voted *Hometown Sweetheart* on the morning show. But Blythe Woods doesn't have me fooled, I remember the piece she did on poor Clyde Mosely, a guy who'd started up his own landscaping business, at least until Big Mouth Blythe came on the scene and did a story about Clyde "starting from scratch." Next thing we knew, poor Clyde got shut down for not having all his paperwork in order.

I take a step forward. Blythe's smile dips as she backs into her camera guy. "And another thing, Blythe. Let's not forget all those things you said about my brother. What was it you called him, a shrimp? Did I get that right?"

"A *pint-sized* shrimp," Zach corrects, shooting me a wink as he chews on a candy bar. "Sorry, Colton."

Colton shrugs. The reporter looks to Dad who's on the phone with the sheriff's office. "Well, I...I must have said—"

Dad steps in but nearly falls down the steps. Colton looks down. "Abby, it's fine, really."

Nope. Not fine. "I think she should issue an on-the-air apology."

Blythe, looking as though she's had enough, shakes her head when the camera guy nods. "Okay, it's go time. We're live."

I look at Dad. "What?"

Blythe turns to the camera and comes alive. White smile, bright eyes. It's like she's a new person. But I know better.

"Hi, we're here on Berkshire Street in East Ridge, where I'm with Abby Clutts, an eye witness to the strange event over at Michelangelo's on Friday..."

Too late, sweetheart.

"Abby, is it true that Lester Mayes..."

A roll of thunder claps as the camera guy looks up. His mouth falls open. "Um, Blythe. Your um, your nose is um..." He motions with his hands. Zach jumps back.

"Holy headlines, look at that schnoz!"

Blythe's hand flies to her nose, which is growing by the inch. She lets out a shriek that sets off car alarms a block away. I close my eyes. I hadn't meant to, not exactly anyway. Oh boy.

Dad drops the phone and it goes fumbling down the steps. "Oh, um, here, let me get you some ice for that."

Blythe screams again, still clutching her microphone as she tears down the steps and sprints for the van. She feels her face with her free hand. The camera guy, who has aimed the camera at the star reporter and captured all of this, turns to us and shakes his head. "She's really sensitive about her nose. I mean... she was...this is...well, gotta run. See ya."

He bundles up a cord and then he's rushing over to Blythe,

assuring her it's not that bad, really, it's the lighting. The angle. The rain.

Colton glares at me. I look away, ashamed because I really, *really* didn't mean to this time. Zach giggles, but it's not so funny anymore. If I can't control my actions, what will I do, lock myself in a tower? I can't trust myself to debate, play chess, spell, or anything involving the pressure of performing. Who knows what might happen. Heck, I can't even be out in public anymore.

I don't dare look at my brother again. I turn away as Dad calls out. I rush up to my room where I slam the door and leap into my bed, burying my head in the pillows, wishing it all away.

I fall into a black void of thoughts, where I'm not in school or at home. I'm somewhere else entirely. Somewhere I've never been but seems familiar, nonetheless. A secluded house in the mountains with a barn in the back. Hawks fly over my head as I'm far away from everyone. I walk for the barn, somewhere I can hide until I'm in control of my emotions and my actions.

It isn't until Mom knocks and peeks in that I pull my head out from beneath my pillow.

"Sweetie, Dad told me what happened. Are you okay?"

"He did?" I wonder what he could have told her. What actually happened or what he thought happened? I rub my eyes and nod. "Yes, I'm okay."

She comes in and sits on my bed. "Want to talk about it?"

I shrug. "Not really. I'm not sure what happened, Mom."

She looks into my eyes. And it's too much. But as I'm about to confess, she strokes my hair and smiles. "Well, they had no business coming here. I'm glad you told her off, just between you and me."

Huh? Did my mom just say that? "Really?"

Mom winks at me. "Your father mentioned some sort of allergic reaction, too. Something with her nose?"

My shoulders drop. I'm such a freak. How many times will I have to explain what I've done, brush it off as some one-off occurrence. I'm not sure how much longer I can do this.

A slight rumble outside shifts Mom's attention to the window. "The storm is coming in," she says. "You know, I used to love watching thunderstorms with Ms. Vereen."

I turn to her. "Who's Ms. Vereen?"

"Huh? Oh, she was my teacher," Mom says with a smile.

"Oh." I smile back. My mom has the softest smile in the world. Looking at it makes everything easier and that much harder at the same time.

"Mom?"

Another rumble of thunder. "Hmm?" She gazes out the window. Her shoulders inch up some, as though she's bracing herself for something unpleasant. I take a deep breath, look at the cup, ready to tell her, show her, to beg for her to help me. But when she turns from the window, her eyes taking me in, all I can do is say,

"I love you."

Chapter 17

I've promised Colton I will be good today. Again. But this time I've promised myself, too. Arriving at school, however, I know it won't be easy.

Dad drops us off because it's dumping rain outside, which means he does his best chauffeur impression. "All right, my lads, steer clear of trouble? Get it Abby, *steer*, clear?"

"Uh, sure, Dad."

It's the kind of day that looks like night. The streetlights glow in the gloom and the headlights from the buses seem out of place. Once we're out of the rain, Colton looks in his bag lunch. "Great, more bread."

Mom's been stuffing us full of the homemade bread lately. Sandwiches, toast, buttered or smeared with cream cheese. "Hey, it could be worse. Remember her broccoli kick?"

"Don't remind me."

Walking inside, our footsteps squeaking in the hallway, the windows are shiny and black as Colton turns to me. "I mean it, Abby. No spells, curses, jinxes. I don't want you even wishing for the rain to stop, got it?"

"Sheesh. Yes, got it, okay?"

I sound more comfortable than I'm feeling. And Colton must know it as he's still staring me down when Lani Andrews comes to the rescue. She adjusts her glasses and smiles at my brother, then me. "Hi, Colt. Hi, Abby."

"Hi, Lani," I say as Colton lights up with a smile. Lani really is the perfect girl for my brother. She's kind of a drama geek, and Colton is too, even if he won't admit it. I shake my head and laugh. She's also a great distraction, as they walk together down the hallway, bumping shoulders.

I stop by Miss Tipton's classroom to say hi, assure her everything is fine, and I will be ready for the opening rounds in a few weeks. I look at the words on the board. Man, I could have killed yesterday. Debate. Chess. Spelling. *Spells.* I have one too many extracurriculars. And it's easy to choose which one needs to go, even if I'm really good at it.

But there's little time to dwell on broken promises, not with Mr. Wolff hawking my every move.

Everyone is buzzing about the news—or at least the part of the segment at my house that was captured on live TV. I'm doing my best to keep my head down when Reagan and her cronies come marching up. Reagan is pointing to her face. "And yeah, her nose, which was already jacked up, totally grew. My cousin saw the footage. I mean, what's up with that? It's like um, Pin, peanut, Penelope...you know?"

I can't help but smile. It's sort of a thrill to hear people talking about what I can do. At least until I'm nearly trampled and one of my backpacks goes falling to the floor.

"Move, child." Reagan says without even looking my way.

I catch my balance and bend to grab my bag. I tell myself to let it go. I really can't do this right now. But then again, who says?

Before I know it I'm calling out to the herd. "Um, excuse me."

All three of them stop and turn. I aim for the middle and shoot Reagan a smile. "The nose thing? I think you meant Pinocchio. He was carved by a woodworker named Geppetto, who lived in a Tuscan village. But then he became a real boy with a penchant for lying—which caused his nose to grow."

Reagan looks to Jordan, who shrugs. Hailey scoffs. But I don't care. I'm sorry, Colton, I tried. I really tried, and they came and knocked me down. So no more letting it slide. I'm emboldened by what I did to Chaz, to Lester, to Mr. Dabney, to Blythe. What I can do to anyone who refuses to show some basic human decency. And Reagan Roebuck is no exception. If knowledge is power, I have nothing to fear.

So when they shake their heads and turn to ignore me, I call out, "Hey Reagan, how's your chin?"

She stops with a squeak. Her groupies stop. This time Reagan aims a searing glare at me, like a nuclear submarine finding its target. "*What* did you say to me?"

She comes clomping back, knocking back her hair. Her preppy little sweater and pleated skirt look tailor made for a teen movie set. Jordan and Hailey wear matching smirks.

"Oh, I was just making sure you were doing okay, after—" I rub my chin and try my best to suppress a smile. "You know?"

"You're Colton Clutts' little sister, right? Shouldn't you be in elementary school or something?"

For a split second I'm once again caught in her pull. It is, after all, only the second time Reagan Roebuck has ever spoken to me. "Yes," I say. "Well, I mean, yes, I'm Colton's sister, but no, I don't belong in primary school. I'm a seventh grader."

She winks at Jordan. "Seventh grader, riiiight." She snaps her fingers. "Oh but, weren't you in the paper recently?" Hailey chuckles as Reagan leans down, her hands on her knees and her eyes wide. "Did that big bad wobber give you nightmares?" she says in patronizing baby talk.

I set my jaw. The tingles flair. Determined to keep things under control, I swallow it down with a smile. "No, actually, he didn't. But I can't say the same thing about your chin. Yowie. I couldn't sleep for days after seeing that gnarly thing."

Reagan straightens. "Excuse me?"

Thunder booms outside. The bell rings. Everyone scatters off to class, a few lingering stares on us. I give Reagan a smile. "Yeah, you have to be careful with warts. I hear they can resurface at any time." I make a show with my hands, the tingles resurfacing, getting away from me. Control gone. Promise broken. "I mean, they can just pop back up out of nowhere."

Reagan's eyes flash. She crosses her arms and scowls. But she doesn't have a chance to respond. Not with her chin giving birth to a whale of a wart.

Her eyes cross trying to focus on the volcano emerging on her chin. Jordan gasps as she and Hailey watch the wart grow and grow and grow and I'm not about to let it stop as it reaches golf ball status on her chin.

She must be too shocked to scream. Jordan whispers, "Oh my..."

I get the wherewithal to turn and get my tail to class. I toss a wave over my shoulder. "Bye, bye, Reagan."

"No, no, no. Not again!"

By the time I walk into Mr. Dabney's class, the entire school hears Reagan's screams. I feign shock, but what I'm really thinking is, *Sorry, Colton. I tried.*

Such a shame, too. Because Reagan Roebuck really is a pretty girl.

THE STORM RAGES outside as the morning announcements begin with a PSA about a bizarre weather system that has settled over our little town. Surprisingly, the surrounding counties are unaffected. The "situation" hovers exclusively over East Ridge.

Mr. Wolff commandeers the announcements and assures us all is well, a gesture that only sets everyone on edge because why would the principal cut in on the announcements if things were normal? They're not, that's why. And now that everyone in the school has heard Reagan Roebuck go shrieking down the hallway, the rumors are rampant.

I can only imagine what Colton will have to say about all of this, but I don't have time to process the thought because a clean shaven Mr. Dabney starts in about a pop quiz. He has the gall to make a joke about getting a refund on grades. He seems awfully cocky for a guy who only recently had a slug removed from his lip.

"So, if we can stop looking out the window and turn our attention to the 'Tariff of Abominations,' maybe we can start to resemble a classroom again."

He saunters up the rows, passing out the quiz, only to stop at my desk. He dangles the page in my face. "What do you say, Abby, think you can bargain your way to an A again?"

Not to be outdone, I shoot him my best smile. "I see you shaved, Mr. Dabney. How was that?"

"Cut it out, Abby," Ahmad whispers from the desk behind me. But I will do no such thing.

"Miss Clutts," Mr. Dabney begins, a slight shiver in his tone. He clears his throat. "My grooming should be the least of your concerns. Perhaps you should focus on the task at hand."

"Sure thing, Mr. Dabney. I'll take a *slug* at it."

His eyes flash. His cheeks redden. The class snickers, and usually I'd be kicking myself, but not today. Promise or not, the contract was flawed from the start. Besides, I'm not little Abby Clutts anymore. And this is *not* the day to try me. I hold his glare with a smile while he stands there, hovering over me.

"Out to the hall, Miss Clutts."

I follow him out of the classroom as the thunder rumbles in earnest. He shuts the door and turns to me. "I don't know what has gotten into you, lashing out the way you have been lately."

He paces about with his hand on his chin, rubbing above his lip where his mustache used to be. I can tell he suspects me, but he's fighting with his instincts. He knows it, I know it. It's laughable even if it's true. On a side note, I must say, I'm really enjoying having the upper hand in these teacher/student meetings.

"Your behavior has been unacceptable at best."

I swallow down the panic in my throat. Since I was three years old, I've never had a teacher tell me I was anything but extraordinary, gifted, a delight to have in a classroom. Now he's calling my behavior *unacceptable*? And he's not finished.

"It's understandable for you to have some social miscues, maturity issues, with your age and all, but enough is enough. Either you pull it together or you can spend your class time with Mr. Wolff. We were discussing your situation, and he feels you could use a bit more discipline in your routine. He thinks..."

A flash at the windows. Seconds later the thunder booms. Mr. Dabney peeks in the classroom, where it's getting loud. He cracks the door, shushes them, takes a step one way then back. I suppose he's just now realizing he's left them unattended with a pop quiz.

"And another thing," he says, getting back to me. "We do not bargain on grades, am I clear?" From somewhere—a locker, the closet—comes a cackle, and his eyes widen. "Abby, are you all right?"

Nope. Not all right, not even close. "How is my behavior unacceptable? And *maturity* issues? Social *miscues*? You can't be serious. I've done everything you've asked, I was simply wondering why you marked question six wrong. And you, all you do is belittle those who dare to ask?"

My voice breaks and I'm hot all over. I've had it. Had it with this school. I've...

Mr. Dabney takes a step back as I approach him. "Aghh, please, no. Don't..."

"Don't *what*, Mr. Dabney?"

"You know, the, the..." His hand flies to his mouth.

I wipe my tears away, my anger winning out. Another cackle and I realize it's me. I'm cackling. "I warned you. I warned you to leave me alone. But you couldn't, could you? You're a bully like all the others, and..."

Mr. Dabney sags to the ground. His bones turning to mush as his skin moistens then fades to an almost translucent sheen before it darkens to a gray with black spots. His voice warbles. It's both disgusting and fascinating watching him turn to goo—to contract and mutate and secrete on the hallway floor. Before my eyes, he becomes what I've always known him to be.

I rub my hands together. Somewhere in the back of my mind I know I should be frightened or alarmed. But I'm not, I'm almost satisfied with what I've done.

"Don't worry, Mr. Dabney. I suggest you go find a puddle and keep hydrated. I would hate for you to desiccate. I'll check back with you later."

Boom. Thunder rattles the windows. The class screams and laughs and I turn from Mr. Dabney who's left a slime trail as he slides off in search of moisture. What I need to do is find Colton and get out of the school while I still have control.

A quick look behind me. Well, maybe the control is gone.

I have, after all, just turned my teacher into a slug.

Chapter 18

I hurry for the gym in hopes of finding my brother, knowing I must stay clear and away from anyone before I cause any more damage. Rain flings itself sideways, pelting the windows in the hallway. Wind gusts bend trees and hurl leaves and debris outside.

Nearing the gym, I slide to a stop at the corner just before the lobby.

Kaspar Wolff roams the quarters in the distance. Maybe not so much roaming but lurking. His shoulders are hunched, his back curved, and he seems to be sniffing his way down the trail. I duck away before he sees me.

Wait. *Kaspar?* Why did I say that? And how did this happen? How did I, Abby Clutts, gifted honors student, become public enemy number one? I suppose it all started when I helped Colton, then it evolved into a war on bullies. Now I've gone after a teacher, again, something that only weeks ago would have been an unspeakable offense. But alas, I'm a one woman wrecking ball, and it's clear I can't help myself. I need Colton.

I'm still crouching when someone shoves me from behind, knocking me to the floor. "Watch it, Clutts."

Turning around, I find Chaz Snead hulking over me. No. *Not now. Please not now, Chaz.*

"Where's your hall pass, half pint?" He sneers at me, totally oblivious to the state of things. It's as though his one purpose in life is to make others miserable. I get to my feet.

"Are you like a hall monitor?" I ask, dusting myself off. I need to lay low, stay out of trouble. But boy did this guy pick the wrong day.

He chuckles. "Yeah, something like that."

When he brushes past me, off to cause trouble somewhere else, I can't resist a parting shot. "Hey, how was gym the other day? Did you have a good, uh, trip?"

He stops, shoes squeaking on the hall floor. "What did you say to me, pip squeak?"

"Ha, *squeak*." I nod to his shoes. My smile spreads. "Well, you took a nice spill on the track, didn't you? It's really been a tough stretch for you," I say, hands behind my back, circling him. I look down to his untied laces. An accident waiting to happen, running around without tying your shoes. "First, the uh, skin thing, then you wipe out on the track. Ouch."

Chaz comes at me, but I've knotted his laces. Splat. He falls like a sack.

Scrambling to stand, he pushes off the floor and plants his feet. He goes for me again but has to catch his fall against the lockers. "You look here, squirt. You think you're funny? You and your freak friends?"

Watching him stagger toward me with his best Frankenstein walk, the scrape on his forehead from his tumble on the track, I should feel bad for poor Chaz Snead. Should, but I don't. I look around for Kaspar or Greenie, but the coast is clear. Time to have some fun.

"Oh, Chaz, I'm not sure I'd be calling anyone a freak, I mean what with all the..."

I gesture to his arms, his skin now the color of Nickelodeon slime. He looks down, sees his arms, and howls.

"No. Noooo! Not again!" His eyes widen as he follows the spread of toxins up his forearms, past his elbows, the fear spreading faster than the green up his arms and legs. He staggers back, the knotted laces measuring his small steps. His chin quivers as he looks at me. "What did you do to me?"

I shrug. "It's more like what you did to yourself, Chaz."

Lightning flashes outside. Boom goes the thunder. Chaz lets out a screech as he looks over his arms, his hands. He holds them up as they glow. With a shrug I free his laces and shoo him away. "Now, run along. I suggest a shower and some self-contemplation. If all goes well you'll be back to your regular sorry self by dinner."

The green keeps creeping up his neck, to his mouth. He folds over, looking at his knees, then comes up hopping around like a boy who wants to leap out of his own skin. Even for someone as dense as Chaz Snead, I truly hope he gets his act together. I'd rather not have to do this again. Or maybe I wouldn't mind so much.

"Ahhh," he turns, realizes his feet are free, and sprints down the hallway. The windows flash again. "Somebody, please help. Help!"

I watch him scurry off, happy to have helped. Then I get back on my way, or, on my rampage as it seems, nearly daring anyone else to try me. I don't even care if Kaspar is around. The lights flicker and the intercom speakers crackle to life. A flick of the wrist as I throw my hands up and the fire alarm sounds.

It's getting too easy.

With the power surge, every classroom becomes a party. Kids out of their seats, bouncing around, some standing on their chairs as the rain lashes against the windows. The teachers seem to have given up. An emergency broadcast blares from the administration office.

"Attention... May I have your attention, please... Abby Clutts, please—"

I cock my head and throw both my hands up. *Zap.* Smoke leaks from the intercom. I turn the corner, and as I pass the nurse's office, the door is open wide and Reagan Roebuck looks up and sees me.

She screams, pointing at me. "There she is! *She* did this to me!" She ducks behind the nurse, not before I see the wart on her chin is now the size of a baseball. "Please, please help me!"

The bewildered nurse has the phone to her ear. "Yes, it keeps growing, it's, yes...hairy." She whisks Reagan back in the office and closes the door. I think she's talking to a doctor.

I keep moving for the gym, knowing Colton is my only hope. Or else I'm going to turn this school into a full blown wasteland.

"Abigail."

Mr. Wolff's voice catches my steps. I skid to a stop before the figure in the shadows. "It's time we talked, don't you think?"

I plant my feet and narrow my gaze. His voice is different. Harsher, deeper, the accent is stronger. The storm rages outside. But I'm not afraid of him or anyone else. "I think the time for talking has passed."

"I wouldn't be so sure," he says, feet clicking on the hall floor. He's unperturbed by the storm, the out of control classrooms, Reagan's screams, green Chaz, or the slug formerly known as Mr. Dabney. It's like he's known all along. I see it in the gleam of his eyes as he steps out of the shadows. It's in the toothy grin on his face. He's been expecting this all along. I clear my throat to find my voice.

"So, you're Kaspar?"

His eyes sharpen. I've taken him by surprise. He recovers quickly. "Quite a storm, wouldn't you say?" He gestures to the window. The lightning flashes against the side of his face. "It's been coming for a while now. And here it is."

The tingles slide down my neck. Although I've been tingling most of the morning, so I've grown accustomed to it. But seeing Kaspar—Mr. Wolff—before me, my confidence drains. He's sizing me up, watching my every move. I'm not sure what might happen next.

"Let's talk about the assembly, remember? When you, uh," he rolls his hand toward me, his fingernails long and sharp. "When you embarrassed me in front of the school. You like doing that to people, don't you, Abigail? You think of yourself as some do-gooder, when you are the one causing all the trouble. You, young lady, are the bully after all."

The tingles in my head are tangled, bunched up, and crowded with no place to go. I take a careful step back, glance toward the gym where an impromptu game of dodge ball is underway.

The black windows, the nighttime atmosphere, nothing seems real anymore. I shake my head. "I'm not. I'm not the bully. That's not true. And the thing at the assembly, I didn't mean to, it just..."

"Ah, I don't believe that, Abigail," he says, plucking something from his sleeve. "Not for a minute. But I will tell you something," he says with a growl. "I *let* that happen. Did you know that? I let you do that to me so I could be sure. And I am sure. Oh, I'm quite sure now."

When he smiles a blast of arctic hits my arms and I'm shivering. I take another step back. "Sure of what?"

His grin broadens. His thin lips do little to conceal his sharp teeth. His eyes now completely black. "That it was you. It is you. Ah yes, you know exactly what you're doing. I suspected something when I first arrived. I felt it. I read your file about how you were a precocious ten-year-old sixth grader. Well," he grins that awful grin. "I had my suspicions, then my doubts. But my instincts were right all along. And then some."

Suspicions. Felt it? "What are you talking about?"

"After the assembly, well, it would seem my premonition was right. It appears you've turned the school into your own grotesque playground. And impressive though it is, as your principal I'm none too happy about it."

Again my shivers turn to tingles. I narrow my eyes at the still smiling Mr. Wolff, when the power flickers on then peters out again. This time it stays dark. The hum of the broken speakers falls silent. The balls stop in the gym. Everything groans to a complete stop. Only the flash of the emergency lights leading down the halls. The clicks of his soles approach as the dark figure closes in.

I try and fail to come up with something, anything, to stop it but I can't. The figure is too strong. Strange as it sounds, I had a feeling something big like this was going to happen all along. He is Kaspar, whoever or whatever that is, he's too strong for me.

Standing before me now he clicks his teeth. "Abigail, I think it is time you come with me." He places a hand on my shoulder.

I shrug him off. Because I can't imagine where he is taking me. "I'm not going anywhere with you."

"Oh, child," he says. "I was afraid it might come to this." His icy hand is on me again, only, the hand is hairy and large. "You think your mother can keep protecting you and the boy? I'm too strong!"

I try to free myself, but he squeezes tighter. I have nothing. No spells, no tingles. I'm about to scream when I hear my name.

"Abby."

I turn, placing my mother's voice but unsure how. But it is her, emerging from the darkness, my mom steps forward. The hand flies off my shoulder, and I bound toward her. She takes me in and I hold onto her tightly. But when I force myself to look back to Mr. Wolff—Kaspar—he's gone.

Vanished.

Mom takes my hand, her eyes focused and determined. She doesn't ask about school or what's going on. The dark figure in the shadows. She only pulls me to her as I try to explain. "Mom, that's Kaspar. The one you were—"

"Come on, Abby, there's someone you should meet."

Chapter 19

"What about Colton?"

The double doors fling themselves open and the storm takes us head on. "He's with Zach. They're safe. You have to trust me, Abby," she yells over the swirling wind, looking back. "I have to get you away from him."

"It's the bread, isn't it?"

Mom pulls me along, hunched over against the wind. "I had to protect the two of you."

"Fortified, huh? And Mr. Wolff? Kaspar?" I need her to say it. I need to know all of this is real. She stops for a moment at the mention of his name. The wind slings the rain sideways. She shakes her head.

"I'll explain to you later."

She takes my hand again and we run, fighting our way through the pounding storm. Mom's van lights up, and we're almost there when a tree limb the size of a utility pole comes flying at us.

"Duck!"

We hit the pavement as the enormous tree flies right over our heads and slams into the school. Mom looks back and we dash for the van.

"Mom, I'm scared. What's going on?"

She points to the van. We hurry inside and she starts the

engine without reminding me to buckle up. Then she catches a wheel as we start down the street.

I look back at the school. The windows flicker as lightning strikes a power line. An explosion of sparks as Mom guns the engine, swerving not to hit the branches and debris in the street. Watching her drive, having led me away from danger, it's like she's become a superhero. Then I remember the floating truck. Lester Mayes.

A shiver runs down my arms. So it's true.

Mom drives, muttering under her breath. I hear the name Kaspar and I grip the door handle. Between what I've done, the principal, my worries about Colton, my mother appearing at my school for a Super Woman rescue mission from my evil principal, nearly being crushed by tree, and the literal black cloud hanging over Peakland Middle School, well, I'm hardly able to catch my breath.

We tear through two red lights before we're on the expressway. The van whines as Mom guns the engine, her eyes only leaving the road for the rearview until we outrun the storm.

The rain lets up, the clouds part, and suddenly it's sunny again. "I really wish you would tell me what's going on."

Mom pats my leg without turning away from the windshield. "Buckle up, sweetheart."

"Mom."

She turns her head but her eyes don't make the trip. "I will, hon. I'll tell you everything. I mean, I think you know, have suspected. But we need to get there first."

There. I watch the rain let up and the streets become only patchy wet as the clouds move until it's like a clear sunny day even as we're drenched. Mom continues to drive in silence. I wipe my face and try to put the chaos in order. No luck. I think of what I've done and my eyes well with tears. Mom reaches for my hand. "I'm so proud of you, sweetheart."

"*What? Why?*"

"Soon."

I give up. We drive for miles, out toward the Blue Ridge Mountains. Eventually she takes a left, and we're on a two lane road, and I'm left with all my questions as we drive out to the country.

It isn't until we're heading down a two track gravel road beneath a canopy of trees toward a big wooden house sitting in a field, settled before the mountains in the distance, that I realize where we're headed. To the house from my daydream.

"Here we are."

I look at her, then the house. "But how?"

She gives me the mom smile, which, I'm happy to see even if I'm getting a little frustrated with all the *soon* stuff. I'm not used to having more questions than answers.

We come out of the trees, and I look at her again as we pull up the gravel roundabout. Wrought iron fencing covered with vines and leaves. Flowers of every color and size spilling from the front garden. A single duck sits in a birdbath. I glance over to Mom as she stops near the porch and kills the engine. She lowers her head to take in the house; a childlike smile about her eyes tells me she's been here before.

I unbuckle my seatbelt. "Okay, so this is the part where you tell me what's going on, right?"

Nothing. She's lost in some sort of trance. There isn't another car in sight, and whatever is feeding the flowers is also feeding the high grass that has nearly overtaken the fence. There isn't another house in sight. Acres and acres of land surround the house, holding more flowers, some scattered trees, and the dusty blue mountains that make for a beautiful backdrop. But I'm not here for sightseeing.

"Well?" I throw my hands up. Mom simply opens her door and steps out. I sigh. "Okay then."

It's at least ten degrees cooler in the foothills. Above the treetops, a hawk glides, his wings spread wide. Mom stares at the house. "Wow, this brings back so many memories."

"I'm sorry, what?"

Mom turns to me as though she'd forgotten I was with her. "Ready for your *tour*?"

My jaw falls like a drawbridge. I look back to the house. The angles, the turret, the slate roof held by huge, used-to-be-white-but-now-peeling-gray columns outside the steps. Perhaps fifty years ago this place was a super nice mansion, but now it looks like something from a movie set. So this is it, the school that doesn't exist. The Piedmont School. But why now? Not sure if she's noticed, but I've sort of destroyed my middle school.

The door opens and I jump back.

A tiny lady steps out to the porch. White hair pulled up in a bun. Old lady dress, sweater, shoes that look like they were assembled by old country cobblers. At first glance it's a tiny old lady, but her eyes shine with youth as she looks out to us and smiles. "Well hello, my dears."

"Hi, Ms. Vereen."

My head swivels. Mom, this lady, Mom, this lady. Then it clicks again. Ms. Vereen. The teacher. I have to double check to make sure it is my mom and not say, a little girl, next to me.

Mom takes the stairs and bends down to hug this lady she clearly knows very well. I cautiously make my way to the steps as Mom lets Ms. Vereen take her hand and look her over. When Mom speaks, her voice is higher, younger sounding. "Oh, gosh, it's been so long. I'm so sorry I canceled the tour. Or that I haven't been out, it's just—" she sighs. "This is all happening so fast."

Ms. Vereen waves her off. "Oh, don't apologize, my dear." She smiles at me. "Oh, now look at this darling."

Darling. My hair is still pasted to my face. My shirt is ripped from where I was nearly decapitated by a flying tree limb. I'm fresh off a duel with my principal. And yet, it makes me blush, this fawning over me.

On second glance, Ms. Vereen moves nimbly. Behind designer glasses, her nearly black eyes bore into me. "And you must be Abby?"

I nod, then remember my voice. "Yes." I clear my throat. "Very nice to meet you."

Ms. Vereen nods to my mother. "Such a polite child."

Mom beams. It's so strange. And here, on the weirdest hour of the weirdest week of my life, all I want to do is scream out for one of them to tell me what's going on. What happened at school? What about Reagan and her chin? Mr. Wolff or, gulp, Mr. Dabney? My throat goes dry thinking of him slithering around the school.

And what are we doing here, with this nice old lady, in a house I recognize, instead of say, a police station? Well, I suppose deep down I know the answer to that. Still, my mother only stands there, fangirling and smiling as Ms. Vereen nods. "Well, won't the two of you come in? I have tea on."

I turn to Mom and mouth, "What?"

Inside, oriental rugs lay on floors that appear polished and gleaming. It smells of cinnamon and bread. My stomach rumbles as I take in the huge staircase that greets us. Mom smiles at it like all she wants to do is go sliding down the banister.

Ms. Vereen shows us to the "sitting room," as she calls it, and says she'll be right there with the tea. There's a large mantel and it smells like an old fire. Books line the walls, black and white photographs—classrooms of little boys and girls. Mom takes it in. I'm too worked up to sit down.

"Mom, are you okay?"

"What? Oh, yes sweetie, it's, umm...well..."

Ms. Vereen returns in a flash. "Okay, here we are." She sets the tray on the coffee table and pours out the tea. "So, Claire, it was such a pleasure hearing from you." She turns to me. "And your daughter, such a striking resemblance to you at that age."

Mom fidgets, gushes a little, and turns to me. "Yes, I suppose so."

"Oh yes. And it's clear she's capable. I can feel it already. I'd say she's beyond capable."

I glance from Ms. Vereen to Mom, Mom to Vereen. "Would someone please tell me what's going on?"

Ms. Vereen adds a drop of honey to her tea, stirs, then sets her gaze on me. Something in her face puts me at ease and yet strikes fear through my chest. She blows gently on the tea, the steam rising over us, taking the shape of a cloud. Mom looks at the floor as though nothing is happening as the cloud turns dark, then pulses with lightning.

Ms. Vereen closes her eyes. "Abby, I know you have many questions. This stage of your journey is both the most exciting and most fearful. But rest assured, you will get the answers you seek. It will require both patience and practice to harness your abilities, not to mention preparation. But I can feel your strength. Remarkable." She turns to Mom. "You were right to bring her."

Mom looks me over with a small smile. We all take a seat. Mom and me on the curved velvet couch and Ms. Vereen in a wingback rocker. I'm about to throw my hands up and storm out to the van when she turns to her teacup and it takes flight. The spoon follows, and soon the honey floats into the air. It twirls and sparkles as it catches the sun's rays and mixes in with the tea.

I gasp. The tingles rush over me as the spoon stirs. But it's different. I'm not tense or scared or spiraling out of control.

Quite the opposite. It's like, for the first time in a long time, I feel like I can breathe.

Mom looks to me. "The other day, with the truck—" She shrugs. "Before the truck. I should have told you, sweetie."

"But..." My comfort turns to anger. "So, you thought *this* would be the way? With," I nod to Ms. Vereen, still with her eyes closed, her cup spinning, the cloud pulsing with light. "And wait, are you saying..."

Mom stopping the truck, showing up at the school. They watch with a smile as it dawns on me. "So, you're like me?"

Mom blinks slowly. "When I was young, I realized I could do certain things." She looks up to all the debris orbiting over us. "These sorts of things. I didn't know who to turn to. Ms. Vereen brought me in, here, with the others, and taught us."

"The others? Taught you? What is this, Star Wars? What others?"

Ms. Vereen hums a song. It's sort of creepy but at the same time familiar. Mom looks around the room. I've never seen her so nervous. "There used to be more. There used to be many more."

"You are the only one now," Ms. Vereen says without opening her eyes.

"Mom, please. So, I mean, I'm really a *witch*. *You're* a witch?"

Mom closes her eyes. "I used to be."

"She was my star pupil."

A slight smile forms on Mom's lips. "But I gave it up, long ago. I thought you'd been spared."

Ms. Vereen's eyes snap open. "Oh no. And not *spared*. She certainly has the *gift*. And I believe Kaspar knows it as well."

"Kaspar?" I look at Mom and throw up my hands. "Mr. Wolff, right?"

Mom nods. She looks to the prism in the window. "Once I

realized Kaspar was here, I knew I had to tell you, but I thought maybe," she looks at the teacher. "We tried some things, but so far he's eluded us." She throws her hands up. "I should have brought you here sooner."

At the school, I'd seen my mother at her strongest. Now, her voice is strained and her face clouds over with doubt. Ms. Vereen soothes her.

"Now, now, dear." The old lady shakes her head. "We mustn't do that. It does us no good to question the past, only learn from it. And the protection spell, wonderful work, dear."

I look back and forth between the two of them. "You mean the bread, right?"

Mom basks in the light of her teacher's praise. But I have questions. I have *so* many. And every answer only seems to bring more questions. I think about the tingles at school. Last year with the spell on Colton's glitter. Thinking of Colton, I nod, turn to the cup, and make it take flight.

"Very good," Ms. Vereen says, her face brightening. She looks again to Mom. "We have a lot to do. She's especially gifted, even with the stubborn streak." She smiles at me. "But I have high hopes for this one."

"I still would like it to be her choice," Mom says before turning to me. "Even though it may be too late for that, now that Kaspar knows."

"Okay, okay. So umm, Kaspar, *is* Mr. Wolff, right? I need to make sure I'm following."

Ms. Vereen nods. "Yes. He has hunted us for quite some time now."

Mom clears her throat. "Your grandmother would not let me practice. I was not to go near Ms. Vereen. She was afraid of Kas —Mr. Wolff. She feared for my safety. But I'm letting you decide, Abby. The choice is up to you."

I don't know why, but I think about my father. "Does Dad know?"

Mom closes her eyes. "I'm afraid not, sweetheart. That's why, when all of this began, back when you helped Colton—"

I whip my head to her. "You knew about that?"

She closes her eyes and nods. "Yes, dear."

"So you know *he* knows."

She nods again. "And I should have talked to you. I was so set on giving you a normal life..." she trails off.

"Yes, you should have. Normal? Nope. I mean, here I've been thinking I'm a freak." I look around. "Which, I'm still not convinced otherwise."

"No sweetheart, you're not a freak. You're...it's...well... I know how hard it can be at school. How mean and cold people can be to those who are different. So once all of this started up again at school this year, I called Ms. Vereen. Because, it appears you've taken yourself to the advanced stages without any help at all."

"The Piedmont School."

Ms. Vereen sets her arms out. "Welcome." She gives Mom a quick glance. "I've heard about what you've done at school, Miss Abby. Most impressive. But dangerous, too."

I'm not over the Dad thing. I get to my feet and throw my hands out. "So you've been lying to Dad all this time? Like, your whole marriage?" I'm not sure why that's what bothers me so much, but it does.

Mom shakes her head. She touches my knee, and it would be a sweet moment if it weren't for a teacup spinning over her head, Ms. Vereen humming over there. "Abby, it's best if we don't tell anyone. Even those closest to us." Her gaze falls to her lap. "At least, that's what I've always thought, until now."

"But I thought you gave it up?" I look from Mom to Ms.

Vereen, back to Mom. "It didn't look like you gave it up on the way to the dentist office the other day."

"Well, motherly instincts." Mom looks to the floor. "And, well," she sighs, her hands in her lap. "I love your father too much to give him up. It was one or the other."

I sigh. "This is heavy."

"It is, it's a lot to throw at you right now. But with Kaspar Wolff in East Ridge, at your school and..." She shakes her head. "How did this happen? It wasn't supposed to happen."

Ms. Vereen sets her tea down. "No, not like this. But I always knew he'd be back. Now, not to be insensitive, but there is little time. Let's review."

I glance up to the steam cloud. And there's Chaz Snead, green as a goblin, roaming the halls, slobbering all over himself. Then Mr. Dabney in a shower stall, soaking up moisture. Ms. Vereen cackles. Mom's eyes are shining when she looks to her former teacher. "A pigment torment. I can't even do that."

Ms. Vereen nods. "Sure you could, had you stayed. But yes, she's beyond her years, certainly. Extraordinary." The cloud zaps. I'm swelling with pride when she turns a teacher stare on me. "However, at present, your emotions are controlling your abilities. We need to fix that."

"Is Mr. Dabney going to be okay?" I ask. "I mean, that second go round I sort of let him have it." I glance at Mom. "Admittedly, I've gotten a little out of control."

"Yes, he'll be absolutely fine. But again, we have plenty of work to do."

I look at the shelves full of potions, the classroom pictures hanging on the walls. Then back to Ms. Vereen. "So, you're like a witch tutor?"

Mom shoots me a look. Ms. Vereen only smiles, still watching me as she takes a delicate sip of her tea. "I am many things. A teacher, a mentor, a guide. A protector. A word puzzle solver. Now, with my help and your, well, prowess, I think we can rid East Ridge of Kaspar Wolff for good." She cocks her brow. "Interested?"

"Well, I'm not so sure I could…"

"Oh, we don't want to *kill* him, sweetheart, it's not what we do." The old lady shoots me a wry smile. "We want to teach him a lesson he'll never forget."

I look around the room. Mom fiddles with her hands in her lap, obviously torn over things. Finally, I shrug. "Well, I've always hated bullies. And it sounds like this Kaspar Wolff guy is the biggest bully of all. So, count me in."

Chapter 20

"**B**ut wait, shouldn't we be worried? About everything at school? I mean, it's sort of a war zone right now," I say.

Mom shakes her head. "The school is fine."

Another steam cloud and I see the halls of Peakland Middle School. The lights are on and everything seems to be in order. Mrs. Tony speaks with Mr. Dabney, who is back in human form again. I look at Mom and she smiles at me. There's Reagan, beautiful again. Chaz Snead is no longer green.

"Well that was fast. Is this, is that real? And where's Kaspar?"

Ms. Vereen nods. "Yes, it is real. The weather disturbance at your school was a clash of...energy, for lack of better terms. Now that you've left, and come here, he will likely follow. But we have some time. Not much, but some."

Mom explains the time portal, how we have a few days to hone my, um, craft, while only minutes will pass in the world outside. I'm not sure I completely understand, but my attention is diverted when Ms. Vereen levitates.

"Now, where is my guide? It's been a while since I've had a new pupil." She floats to the top shelf, her feet five feet in the air.

Mom smiles at me. I lower my voice. "Please tell me I'll be able to do that."

Mom pats my knee. "You already can." She sets her teacup down and looks at the floor. "It's been years for me, however."

Mom closes her eyes and takes a super big breath, like when she's doing yoga in the living room or after Colton or Dad breaks a dish. And then she's light as air, hovering with Ms. Vereen. She looks down, her eyes wide and shining.

I shake my head. "Mom, I can't believe you never told me."

"I'm telling you now, Abby."

"Here it is," Ms. Vereen pulls a dusty book from the shelf. Mom continues to watch her own feet dangle. Ms. Vereen looks at me. "Now, Abby. Up."

Up? What am I, a Labrador? "I uh, I can't fly."

"We're not flying, we're simply bending gravity."

"I thought you used a broom?"

"Nonsense. Now, come up here."

"I can't."

"Sure you can. Now come."

I get to my feet and hop about three inches off the floor. "See?"

Ms. Vereen smiles at Mom. "And we thought she was gifted."

Mom giggles. I glare at the old lady. Tingles spread down my back and my body feels light. Ms. Vereen whispers, "There we go," just as I leave the floor.

"What in the..."

Two feet, three, then four and soon I'm eye level with Mom. I turn left, then right, then spread my arms and spin.

"Well, that was fast." Ms. Vereen taps the book, about the size of a small briefcase. "Now, this way. There's lots to do."

We start with a review. Things I've already done. From there we spend the day in the book. And it's a good thing I like books because Ms. Vereen was right, we cover a lot of ground.

It's also nice to have my mom to myself. The only time she ducks out is to call Dad and explain that we have some extracurricular things to do—not exactly a lie.

The levitation comes easy. Basic physics, drag and pull, and it's not even lunch when I'm better at it than Mom. Ms. Vereen explains the tingles, which are actually electric pulses from the brain, zaps triggered by emotions that interfere with my trigeminal nerve. After working on some breathing techniques and muscle patterns, it isn't long before I'm a girl in complete control of her abilities.

Then we have some fun. Outside, Ms. Vereen sets up three jars about thirty yards away. She places a feather in one jar and instructs me to protect it at all costs while destroying the empty ones. The only catch is, they hurl insults at me. They call me a baby and a whiner and Mom whistles and claps her hands to distract my focus. Sure enough, it's tingle time, and I destroy everything.

"Sticks and stones, Abigail," Ms. Vereen says.

"It's Abby."

She shoots me a wicked smile. "Very well."

We set up again and again and she continues to call me Abigail until I'm able to push back on the tingles. Ms. Vereen says it's important I learn to block out my emotions. The anger, the vengeance. Basically everything I've been doing at school. Soon, the jars shatter and explode but I manage to keep the feather jar safe. I even turn my back and cross my arms. What can I say? I'm a show off.

As dusk settles over the mountains, Mom gets fidgety. By then I'm floating all over the place, flying, spinning, spelling. I can't help but wonder what Colton would make of all this. Or Dad. I mean, I'm moving boulders, felled trees. I even lift the van off the ground to prove I'm capable.

I declare myself ready for Kaspar Wolff.

Ms. Vereen has her doubts. "Not yet, dear."

I roll my eyes. "Why don't we all go, the three of us? We would be unstoppable."

Ms. Vereen looks at Mom. I watch this exchange. "What?"

"I'm an old lady, sweetheart, and well, I'm not as strong as I once was."

But there's something else. We go back inside and Ms. Vereen pulls out another book. She opens to the back, finds a photo, and pulls it out to show me. It's brown from age, the edges worn and tattered, but it was taken in front of the same house I'm standing in now. Four students, Ms. Vereen off to the side, proud. She points to a boy about my age, the one standing closest to her. Mom's face goes tight, as though she knows the story.

"Kasper Wolff was a special case, to say the least. He arrived out of nowhere, seemingly, when I caught him stealing one of my chickens. He was a small boy, bony and filthy, but it was clear from the start he was special. I took him in and he quickly became my top pupil. Oh, I had great hopes for him. He was to become my assistant."

"He doesn't seem like the assistant type."

"Well, no. And he too was impatient." She smiles at me. "Always impatient. He was temperamental and never wanted to complete his lessons. But he had great abilities. Abilities I'd never seen before, haven't seen again until...today." She gives me a weak smile. "But his aspirations were less than noble."

"So he became a middle school principal," I say, trying to lighten the mood.

"He began showing darker tendencies. Bad signs."

For the first time since we've met, Ms. Vereen looks— vulnerable. Almost frightened. "I did some things I regret. I only wanted to protect everyone."

Mom sets an arm around her old teacher's shoulder. "You did the right thing."

"I thought it was the right thing."

I throw my hands up. "What? What happened?"

"Well, like I said, he became angry, disillusioned. But then he started recruiting my other students for his own school—a school with less than noble intentions. Well, it was clear he was no longer one of my students. And so, I banished him."

"Banished?"

"Or so I thought. He took to the barn."

I laugh. "You put him in the barn?"

Mom and her teacher exchange looks again. Ms. Vereen frowns. She shifts in her seat and I can see the memory is hard for her. "I knew his strength, or, at least I thought I did. I feared a mutiny was at hand. Still, I tried to persuade him to do the work, to follow the lessons. But he was changing. I'd never seen anything like it. The chickens disappeared. The howling started. He stalked the house for years, I could feel it, I knew he was around. And so I tried once again to reason with him, to convince him to return and do things the right way." She closes the book. "But it was far too late then."

"Wait. Whoa. So my new principal was a student of yours. And then you *banished* him and he changed into, what? A wolf? And now he's returned as *Mr. Wolff?* Kind of bold, wouldn't you say?"

She nods grimly. "I don't know if he changed or if it's simply who he was all along. But I did know he would return, I just didn't know he would be so strong, so vengeful." Ms. Vereen turns her head and pulls back her hair. A scar runs down her cheek to her neck line.

My smile drops. "He did that?"

Ms. Vereen nods. Mom slides over, looking at our teacher. "I can't risk it. I can't put this on her."

"Mom, I can do it. I've already faced him once." My voice breaks, along with my confidence. I turn away from the ugly scar, remembering how easily he'd overpowered me.

Ms. Vereen frowns. "No, I wouldn't ask you to do that, Claire." She looks at me then back to Mom. "Then again, he would have already taken her had he been able to. Your spell worked. I'd say you've still got it, my girl."

Mom strokes my hair the way she used to in the mornings before school, when I was afraid about skipping a grade and worried about the older kids. She'd sing lullabies and tell me I was special. Special. I always thought she said it to put me at ease. Now she's humming again. Then she stops.

"So I'll go with her."

Ms. Vereen smiles. "Power in numbers. I like it."

Mom lowers her brow. "What are you thinking?"

Ms. Vereen looks down to her book. The pages turn by themselves. "Well, just that there is something, though it's more legend than anything else. And it might be too dangerous." After all, I'm not a young woman anymore, and you dear, haven't exactly honed your abilities over the years. And she, while strong beyond belief, is merely a child."

She says the last part more like a dare than suggestion. And it works. Mom edges closer, staring at her former teacher. "You're not talking about... I mean, is that even real?" She looks around. Ms. Vereen watches me as Mom fights with whatever she's trying to say. She takes a breath. "Do you mean a Centroid Formation?"

Ms. Vereen shuts the book. "Well, Claire, I'm impressed you even know the name. And so I suppose you probably know it hasn't been done in a thousand years or more. I've never even seen one performed. I've only read about them."

"Um," I glance from Mom to Ms. Vereen. "Why are we talking Geometry right now?"

Ms. Vereen smiles at me. "Then again, my gut tells me she's the one, Claire, the point. You know it's true."

Mom stops stroking my hair. "Yes, I know. In a way, I've always known."

Chapter 21

While Mom and Ms. Vereen have a private chat in the sitting room, I wander throughout the house, taking in the photos and old furniture. Running my hands over the furniture or the railing, I can almost feel my mom's past in these room. It's like I hear her telling secrets, giggling, running around with her classmates.

But then she stopped coming here. Why? How could she? She mentioned my grandmother, did grandma have this too?

This. Powers. Spells. Whatever it is. And Dad doesn't know. When all of this started, I thought Dad and Colton were the "special" ones. We would laugh about the Clutts family curse, how they were so clumsy they could hardly walk. But now, thinking of what I need to do, where all my spells and plans have gotten me, maybe I'm the one who's cursed.

I let my fingers skip over the spindles of the staircase. I step outside and walk around the yard. The sky is a vibrant blue, the sun warm on my arms. I roam toward the back where everything is overgrown, untended. Wind chimes are left muted in the still air. The bird baths are dry as a desert.

I drift beneath a large trellis covered with vines. Stone statues and benches are nearly swallowed in the tall grass. A sun dial, a moon goddess, some sort of hieroglyphs on the rocks that line the old iron fence. On one of them sits a triangle. Three figures at the points—the lines intersecting at the medians. A weathervane spins slowly even as there is no breeze. My mind works the math. *Centroid Formation.*

Past. Present. Future. The figures on the stone harness their power from the angle they've formed, as though leveraging their power. Whatever is caught in the center of gravity—something with four legs—is powerless to their intersecting streams. Chills run down my arms.

I jump out of my thoughts, ready to rush in and tell Mom and Ms. Vereen how ready I am when the old barn in the distance steals my attention.

Its weathered planks are warped and dilapidated. The metal roof shows rust around the edges. Ms. Vereen's words about Kaspar Wolff rattle in my head as I start for it, pulled toward the barn, leaving my discovery behind.

I'd be lying to say I'm not afraid to face him. But with Mom and Ms. Vereen at my side, I know we have to try. Because I'm more afraid for what could happen if he were to turn Peakland Middle into his own school with his own students.

Thinking of the school reminds me of the wreckage I left behind. What if the entire town were to fall like that? What would stop him from going further, his power growing until he was in complete control of the world?

I'm drawn to the barn as I think about how Kaspar Wolff roamed these same grounds. The wind chimes come to life as the wind picks up, blowing my hair around, pushing the squeaky weathervane in circles. I make my way toward the old structure, to see where Kaspar went after being banished. I aim my eyes at the barn doors and they swing open. I remind myself I can't go around doing that out in the world.

It's dark. The floor is covered with straw. I can make out a few empty stalls as a faint whistle of wind blows through the cracks. I turn toward some rustling in the far corner. "Hello?"

My steps creak on the dusty planks. My feet lead me inside

to the dark, the only light is that filtering through the gaps in the boards.

"Hello?" I say again, blinking as my eyes adjust to the dark.

When I look back to the house it seems miles away. I never told Mom or Ms. Vereen I was going outside. But I sense someone here.

I feel movement in the corner. "Who's there?" I call out, trying to coax whatever it is out of hiding. I take a step inside, then another. The barn doors slam shut behind me.

I whirl around with a scream.

"Abigail. I knew you would come."

I lose my breath. My chest tightens. "What's going on?"

Such a stupid question. I need to speak strongly, to prove I'm not afraid of him. But I am afraid of him. And it's messing with me.

More creaking steps in the dark. I can almost hear his grin sliding up his teeth. "You know what. Don't play dumb with me now. It seems you are the teacher's pet."

I can't do this alone. I turn for the door but it's stuck. I back away and throw up my hands, trying to force it open with my powers, but it doesn't budge. "Leave us alone."

The planks creak with his steps. "I'm afraid I can't do that. You know, I used to come here to get away from it all. When the other students would tease me for being smaller, younger, too naïve. I'd wander out and spend time in the darkness. Just me and my thoughts and my…" A blast of arctic air hits me in the face. "My craft."

I stumble back, wiping at my face. I still can't see him. But he's close. Still talking like he's my principal. "And then, once Ms. Vereen banished me, well, I had no choice. I was not like the others, couldn't pretend to be. But you, you understand, don't you? We're not that different at all, are we?"

"Yes, we are."

His steps circle me. And his breathing. I spin around, looking left, right, up, and down, but I don't see him. "She's not what she seems, Abigail. Oh, she'll teach you, but as soon as you question her, start thinking for yourself, *poof*, you end up here."

The fear wins out. I try the door again. No luck. The tingles come hard. My mind reels and my breaths are shallow. It feels like I'm spinning in the dark. Blinking out of it, I spot a shadow, but then it's gone. I force myself to stay strong, to keep myself together. I call out to him. "I know what you're doing."

His steps creak. "This was my home for many, many years. And like you, they always said I was too weak, too small, too... emotional. But what is the world without emotion, Abigail? We need to feel what they do to us. We need to use it, harness it."

"Stop saying *we*. We are not alike!"

He clicks his teeth. "And yet, in the end it was not me who was weak, but them. Oh, yes, I rose to the occasion, but our teacher," he pauses to let it sink in, *Ms. Vereen*, "she was jealous of my power. She never thought I was quite ready. She never trusted me. She feared me, Abigail."

"What do you want from me?"

"Oh, little girl. You have such great gifts at such a young age. And like me at your age, I forget you don't know much at all about this, now do you? I suppose Ms. Vereen has told you how awful I am. That the blame lies with me. That I tried to ruin her. When in fact, the opposite is true."

Another step and the shadow looms closer. It's dark, but I make out a snout. Gleaming red eyes. I stifle a scream.

"What kind of teacher would turn their back on a student, Abigail?"

"One who knew you were dangerous."

"She didn't think I could do it. How did she put it?" Another click of the teeth. I can picture him walking around, head down, hands behind his back. "Oh yes, she said I was too impulsive. That I let my emotions control my decisions. Does any of this sound familiar?"

"No." I force the word from my mouth. But didn't she say that to me? Something like it at least? And now I'm locked in the barn. *Imprisoned.*

"She's using you to stop me."

"No."

"Aren't you tired of being a little girl? Isn't that why you started doing those things at school?" He sounds like the principal again. But he's not, I can feel it. He's lurking in the dark. I try to stay with him, but he's too elusive.

"And your classmates. Oh, little Abby. That's what they say, right? Oh and your own family, how they love Colton, don't they? Here you are, changing the world, and they dote on that poor dumb boy."

"He's not dumb! And they don't. They..." My mind wanders, to all the expectations of excellence. The awards. How I bring home A after A and it goes unnoticed. At dinner, how my parents praise Colton while I'm skipping through grades. The tingles hit. Kaspar laughs. I take a deep breath. I have to get a grip.

He's only trying to pit me against everyone. Even my own family. I can't let him trick me. And more importantly, why? Why does he want to trick me? I continue to breathe, to fight off the surge of anger in my chest. Because he needs me, that's why.

I force myself to speak calmly. "What do you want?"

"I want you to join me, Abigail. I've watched what you can do, admired your temper. A thing of beauty, it is. I've seen it in action. We can do so many great things together."

I feel my confidence returning. "Great things, like what?"

"Everything. You need to grow. And I can help you. Otherwise..."

A flash in the barn temporarily blinds me. A boom moves the ground beneath me. Everything collapses but doesn't.

Confidence gone.

"What are you doing?" I shriek, shielding myself as I wait for a beam to fall. For the whole structure to come down. And it does, only not like I was expecting. The walls fade, and I gasp as the barn and everything in it spins then stops. I blink into a wash of light that's warm on my skin. Suddenly, I'm in an auditorium.

An auditorium I know well. Last year's spelling bee.

I find my balance, but Kaspar is gone. Or he's not visible even as I feel his presence lurking. I gasp, seeing a version of myself on stage. The other spellers stand obediently in the background. *No, not this. Anything but this.* I watch myself fidget next to Tanvir. I remember how I didn't want to wear a stupid dress but Mom insisted. I look eight.

The host blinks his eyes. He looks at me. "Embarrass."

No. No. No. I whirl around and scream. "Make it stop."

Kaspar's laugh finds my ears. "Oh, Abigail. How could you? I'll bet you were, embarrassed. It's shameful, really."

I turn, tingles coursing through my bloodstream as I rush onto the stage. Tanvar, other me, no one seems to notice when I stamp my foot and scream at the host. At myself. Out into the audience. "Come out and face me! Face me now!"

"That's it, Abigail."

A deep laugh crashes into me from miles away before a *bang bang bang* on the barn door. Faint voices call out. "Abby. Are you in there, Abby?"

"Yes. And he's here!" I call out, just in time to see myself lose the spelling bee. All because I forgot an R. How. How?

"Abby, stay away. We're coming. Don't let him get you."

Oh. I'm sorry, that's incorrect. The correct spelling is...

I grab the sides of my head. My pulse thumps in my ears.

It's too much. Kaspar eggs me on as anger and resentment swell. The emotions take over. The banging gets louder. The thumping of my heart increases. Kaspar steps out and I see him for what he is, a monster.

"Last chance, Abigail. Your mother can't protect you now." His voice is more of a growl. His nose a snout and his teeth are long and gleaming.

But I'm too mad to be scared. "It's Abby."

I close my eyes and plant my feet. I summon any and everything I have. All that I've learned. I open my eyes but Kaspar only laughs, openly, proudly. A terrible, guttural howl of a laugh.

"Oh, please, you little child. You don't think you can hurt me, do you? That day at the assembly, I let you have that. And the spelling bee, consider this your first lesson. I'm revealing your weakness. How easy it is to rattle you. You have no chance against me."

Again I try to stop him. I use all the tricks. The feather in the jar. The breathing techniques. Levitation. What I've learned. But nothing seems to faze him, and I'm about to throw something when the door blows off the hinges and falls to the ground, zapping the bogus stage.

The lights, the spelling bee, my brightly lit failure flush away. Mom and Ms. Vereen appear as two silhouettes against the sunlight. I'm so happy to see them that I lose track of Kaspar, until he growls again.

Kaspar looks up and an unspoken conversation wages between him and Ms. Vereen. I need to act, to strike before he does something, but Mom shakes her head, her eyes pleading with me to stay put.

A strong hand finds my back, nearly paralyzing me. My anger, the tingles, the thump of my heart gives way in Kaspar's grip. He's strong, and his voice is so deep and powerful it hums through my chest. "The school," he bellows. A piece of the barn falls to the hay. "The world. The existence of things to come. If she won't join me, well, I can't have her running around mucking things up for me."

"She won't join you. She's not like you. She's..." Ms. Vereen smiles at him. "Good."

Mr. Wolff releases me and charges toward her. Mom moves, taking position, and I realize what's going on. The formation. We're going to do it. And he's almost in place.

Anger radiates off him like heat as he looms over the little woman before him.

"You think, you think *she* is good, or formidable? This... child? You've never given me the respect I deserve. You were jealous of me!"

His voice grovels. I slip into the third position. The point. But nothing's happening. He's grown before my eyes. He's hardly even human anymore—if he ever was. And still, Ms. Vereen only smiles. "Oh, Kaspar, no, I was never jealous of you. I hoped great things for you. I made a mistake, that's all."

"Nonsense!" Kaspar roars. He throws his head back, kicking a piece of the barn into the abyss.

I roll my neck. My mind is mush. My body aches and I'm tired, ready to drop where I am and sleep. The spelling bee. All my failures. All the things I cannot do, including the Centroid. Maybe Ms. Vereen was right, it can't be done. I move again and Mom motions for me to hold while Ms. Vereen remains calm, her voice more suited for tea time than this beast before her.

"But the girl. She is more than formidable. She's perhaps my finest student yet."

Kaspar's eyes flash. A trembling comes over him. He laughs, howls as though it's the funniest thing he's ever heard. His skin is covered by a dark coat of hair.

"I'm afraid it's true," Ms. Vereen nods. The winds pick up, lightning flashes. Kaspar bellows and throws the old lady back.

"Ms. Vereen!" I call out. I leap over the fallen beam and take a step toward Kaspar when Mom calls out for me to get back. But it's not me who needs protection. Because I am formidable. And I've had enough of this big bad bully.

I stand before the great Kaspar Wolff and summon the emotions, every cell of power within me. I use the anger for strength, my youth for energy. I use all my past failures for knowledge. He will not win this time. But on my own, he's too strong. His laughter knocks me back.

"Oh, little girl. This is only the beginning. Wait until you see what we can do!"

When I stumble back, I see Ms. Vereen. *The Past*. Mom. *The Present*. And now, realizing what's happening, I duck away from Kaspar and become the point. *The Future*. I know I'm in the right place as a powerful surge of current moves through Ms. Vereen, charges through Mom, and then courses through me and it's all I can do to hold it.

Kaspar, only now seeing what we've done, laughs. But his laugh betrays him. He spins around wildly. "No, it will never work."

Ms. Vereen looks up just as a bolt of lightning comes down through the barn. The charge knocks through Ms. Vereen, then to Mom, then it explodes in my chest. Without another blink, the three of us throw out our hands. And there, caught in the point of concurrency, is Kaspar Wolff.

He rolls his neck and lets out a ragged scream, fighting and struggling against our current. The barn shakes as the gale force winds come down from the mountains. A windstorm of dirt and rock and debris hits the walls. My mother screams, Ms. Vereen lets go with an impressive string of expletives. I breathe in, my chest swelling with the storm and courage. But it's slipping away, knocking me back. I can't hang on much longer.

"Keep fighting, Abby," Mom calls out over the wind. I close my eyes tight and use what I've learned. The storm, the lightning, the weathervane spinning furiously in midair. I don't so much tame my nerves as use them to generate power. I use it all, my swirling emotions, my fears and worries and failures—how I'm too small, too short, too little—while everything falls apart around me. The power builds to a crest before I close my eyes and gather myself.

All of this happened with a simple spell, playing with Colton's stage props. Then to my loss of control at school, the principal finding ways to call me out, seeking me out. I stand tall, and when the tingles come, I use them. I bundle them into a force to be reckoned with. I am in complete and total control.

When Kaspar turns to me, teeth gnashed, fur up, his deep growl rolling with the thunder, I stand my ground. I remember the assembly. I beat him once and now, I close my eyes again as he tries to leap out of our intersection, I unleash everything I have at him.

I only hope it's enough.

Chapter 22

I blink my eyes into the sun, coughing up dust and dirt into the haze. It looks as though a tornado has ripped through the barn. I feel like a tornado has just ripped through the barn. Splinters of wood, siding, and beams lay scattered among the straw and hay bales, the wreckage of the old fence. But I'm alive, I think.

My eyes adjust at the sight of my mother hovering over me, stroking my hair.

"Sweetie. Are you okay?"

I prop myself up on my elbows. The clouds are moving fast, speeding away like they're being chased by the breeze. Only the lazy squeak of the weathervane that's landed on the chicken coop reminds me where I am. Another coughing fit hits as I wipe my forehead. A flash of Kaspar lunging for me.

His eyes, those teeth. I jerk myself up and look around. Mom takes me in her arms. She hugs me tightly then picks straw out of my hair. She's got some in hers too.

Are you okay? It's what she said to me after the spelling bee. But nothing was okay then. I thought I'd failed. I didn't know how to deal with failure. But now, as I squint into the sun and find my mom's face, I realize I'm okay. It's okay to fail. To learn from failure.

I nod, still looking around the wreckage. "Is he...gone?" Dead, vanquished, defeated?

It's eerily quiet. Only the hawk circling above our heads, calling out. Mom shrugs. "I think so."

Slowly we get to our feet. We start looking for Ms. Vereen. I gasp, remembering Kaspar lunging for her. The beams crashing from the roof. I'm fearing the worst when I hear some shuffling. Mom and I follow the sound to a pile of debris. "Ms. V!"

I'm nearly in tears as Mom and I start throwing stuff to the side. I send a beam flying using only my eyes. There are blocks of concrete and splintered wood and a boulder that must weigh a thousand pounds. But Ms. Vereen is tougher than she looks. I watch in awe as the old teacher gets to her feet with a cough.

She looks around, places her hands on her hips, and winces as she arches her back. "Ah, much better. Well, I suppose I can knock Centroid Formation off the bucket list. Once is enough though, would you ladies agree?"

Mom and I laugh. Ms. Vereen's glasses sit crooked on her ears, broken on one side, while her dress is ripped in places. She rolls her neck and cracks her knuckles. "Sorry ladies, it's been a while," she says, twisting one way then the other. "As in, never. That. Was. Amazing!"

She's a bit wobbly, and I notice a gash on her arm, but she's in good shape, all things considered. One last roll of her neck and she looks around, thinking what we're all thinking: *Where is he?*

Mom turns left, then right, shielding the bright sunshine with her eyes. "Where did he go?"

"Maybe he's gone," I say, my voice full of hope. I can't imagine another round if he's lurking around here somewhere. All I want to do is climb in bed and sleep for days.

Ms. Vereen doesn't seem so worried. In fact, she looks me over closely, takes my chin in her hand.

"All this time, you were the one. The point. It's remarkable. Just remarkable."

I'm about to remind her it was a team effort when the unruly bray of a donkey steals our attention.

Mom smiles. "Ms. V, you don't have a donkey, do you?"

The teacher's smile lights up. "I believe I do, actually."

I look at Ms. Vereen, then to Mom. "No way."

We follow the sound, wiping ourselves down, picking debris from our hair, coughing as we reach the pens. Amid torn and ripped clothes is a rather large donkey, chewing on some weeds. Ms. Vereen smiles. Mom shakes her head in disbelief.

"No."

We approach the donkey. Ms. Vereen rubs its head. "Kaspar, is that you?"

The donkey snorts, this time showing teeth. He kicks his back legs in the air, and it's then I see the white slash just above the left eye. Mom looks at me and laughs. "I'd say we found your principal."

Ms. Vereen lowers her head and stares the donkey in the eyes. "Yes, that's him all right." She turns to me. "Young lady, I believe you've just done what a generation of witches were unable to do."

I look at Mom who has a dirt smudge on her cheek, then to Ms. Vereen, all ripped up and bleeding. "I think we all did it."

Mom launches into me with a hug. Ms. Vereen joins in. The donkey head butts the fence post. I look around at the wreckage of the barn. Ms. Vereen says she'll have it rebuilt. Mom looks at me.

I ask, "What about school?"

Ms. Vereen smiles. "I think your school is going to be fine from here on."

Chapter 23

Colton is lecturing me on "being more careful" as we walk to school on a bright and crisp fall morning. I nod, bite my tongue, think about muting him with a spell, but otherwise enjoy the sunny morning. Besides, he's awfully full of himself as he skips along, jabbering about how he searched the halls and stairwells up and down for me when the school closed due to the freak power surge.

He brings me up to speed about the school, the town, how Mr. Wolff has already bailed. Talk about sticking it out—the guy didn't even make it a semester.

Told-you-so's or not, it feels great to have Colton by my side again—at least until Zach comes running to catch up.

"Well, if it isn't Peakland Middle's most notorious criminal."

I glance at Colton, then shrug. "In the flesh."

"Wow," he says. "Abby Clutts serving in-school suspension. What's next, you going to knock off a liquor store?"

"Ha ha." I attempt to laugh it off, but it's true. Our newest new principal, Mrs. Tony, gave me three days in-school suspension for skipping class. Even after Mom explained it was an emergency. Considering I did turn my teacher into a slug, I thought it best not to press the issue. Zach continues with his one-man comedy routine.

"So tell me, when you make the license plates..."

"*Ba-dump, bump.* Are you done?"

Zach shakes his head. "Oh no. Not even close."

Considering my wrath the other day, Ms. Vereen was right, all seems well at Peakland Middle School. The school has been cleaned and sanitized. Cleared by safety officials. The admins have issued a statement assuring parents everything is well. Principal Tony—my punishment excluded—has welcomed the students back with an open door and an open mind.

And if I didn't know any better, I'd assume it's all a dream as the three of us enter the school. No signs of chaos. All the lights are on and the floors shine. I find Chucky waiting for me, and together we walk down the hallway.

My steps slow and I hold my breath as Chaz Snead rushes up to us. But it's all precautionary, there's nothing to fear.

Chaz sets a hand on Chucky's shoulder. "Hey Chucky, how are you? Lovely day outside, isn't it?"

Befuddled, Chucky looks at me. I smile and shrug as he slowly turns to Chaz, who's eagerly awaiting his answer.

"I'm good?"

Chaz nods. Gone is that arrogant smirk, the wisecracks and nicknames. Instead he nods and smiles and seems genuinely interested in my friend's wellbeing. "Great. Have a great day, both of you. Well, see you around!"

Colton eyes me carefully. Chucky scratches his head. "What was that all about?"

I watch Chaz spin and bounce off, waving to people in passing, smiling. I'd never believe it if I weren't watching it myself. "I think he's turned over a new leaf."

Colton shakes his head. "So weird."

"Yeah. I think something must be going around."

Colton shoots me a look. "What's that supposed to mean, Abby?"

"It means," I pause and take a deep breath. "I think

Peakland Middle School has finally rid itself of whatever was plaguing it. I think we're all going to be okay."

Colton's careful gaze lingers on me. I know what he's thinking. Last night we had a family discussion. Mom with Dad, Mom and I with Colton and Dad at the dinner table. We covered everything, almost. Mom thought it might be too much to ask them to understand Centroid Formations. She also made it abundantly clear that I am under no circumstances ever to list my classmates or teachers as *Targets*. Fair enough, I promised open dialogue, self-control, and to keep working with Ms. Vereen every day after school.

Dad, in his usual easygoing way, took the news well. He went on about how he knew I was special all along, although I could tell he was a little bummed about his *Out on a Limb* memoir. Just thinking about having it all out in the open brings a smile to my face.

Maybe it's just me, but the school seems cleaner, brighter, the sun streams through the school windows a little warmer and stronger. Jada's last big story focused on Mr. Wolff and his strange disappearance. How she wasn't going to rest until she got to the bottom of things. Keep digging, Jada. You won't find a thing.

We're a few steps into the lobby when Reagan Roebuck and friends come strolling up to us.

"Oh my gosh, Abby. I *love* that shirt. It really sets off your eyes."

Zach, Chucky, and Ahmad stand gaping as Reagan raves over my shirt, glasses, both book bags, and my shoes. I bow graciously, the warmth rising to my face as Jordan and Hailey nod in agreement. I'm adorable, simply adorable. And then they're off, greeting others with smiles and compliments.

Zach slides closer. "Abby, what did you do?"

I'm still wiggling my toes in my shoes as Colton shakes his head. I say, "Nothing, I promise."

He eyes me closely, but I'm telling the truth. He shrugs into his book bag strap. "Okay, I'm getting to class before this gets any crazier."

Mr. Dabney greets the class with a boisterous hello. He's clean shaven, and he's lost the black-framed eyeglasses. He shows no sign of being a slug. It's almost like I imagined the whole thing.

But I didn't. And now I know who I am, and I'm proud of the person I've become. And the changes at our school are almost magical. Detention or not, our new principal seems to actually care about her students. She's already scheduled a Fall Bash, complete with hayrides and farm animals. I hear there's going to be a donkey.

"Well, hello, Abby."

"Hi, Mr. Dabney."

He hands my paper back, corrected with a big fat A. "Wonderful job, as always."

Ah. All is well again.

Well almost. There's still one more thing.

At the end of school, in the lingering minutes before I start pulling my after school suspension time, I walk into spell study to announce my plans. I will not be entering this year's bee.

Someone gasps. Mrs. Tipton looks me over. "Abby, are you feeling okay?"

I shrug. "Yeah, actually. I am. I might return another year, who knows. But for now, I don't need to prove anything else to anyone. I'm also taking a hiatus from debate and chess. Life is short, I've learned, I shouldn't put so much stress on myself. Besides, I have other, new extracurriculars to home in on."

Mrs. Tipton looks me over with a small smile. "Something seems different with you."

I smile back. She couldn't be more correct. "Yeah? Different is good. It took me a while to realize that."

"Very well."

I leave the class and whisk off to suspension with my chin high and my shoulders square. Yes, I'll miss spelling and debate-the competition runs in my veins. But it's not all that runs through me. I have big things ahead of me. I'm excited for what's to come. I'm ready to hone my craft at Ms. Vereen's after school every day. And even though I've promised Mom no more spells at school, I will stay vigilant and ready at all times.

Who knows what else is lurking out there?

My path has changed. This is who I am, who Mom is. And with this ability comes great responsibility. I have to choose my time wisely.

After all, I have a donkey to train.

LOOKING FOR MORE?

Turn the page for a sneak peek at how it all began in *Fairy Dust Fumble* (July 2021, Immortal Works).

It's game day. I throw on my powder blue Panthers jersey and tuck it into my jeans. Only it's too bulky and it bunches up at the waist, and so I untuck it but then it looks like a dress. I settle on something in between, the half-tuck, then check myself out in the mirror. I work on my scowl until I accidentally bite the inside of my cheek.

I tell myself again that things are fine, just fine. And for three or four steps down the hallway things *are* fine, right up until I find my mom and my little sister in the kitchen, huddled at the table, shaking their heads and stifling laughs.

My little sister reaches out to the phone—my phone!—and touches the screen. "See, right there. He tips forward and from there it's all over."

"Poor thing," Mom offers. My sister shrugs, then touches the screen to resume the video. Sure enough, like an old cartoon, a clash of cymbals followed by the tinkly clatter of xylophone keys fills the kitchen. Only this is no cartoon they're watching.

I step out from the doorway. "Hey, what are you guys doing with my phone?"

They whirl around, eyes wide with caffeine and guilt. And just like that, any hopes last night was some strange dream that left my back sore is squashed to bug guts.

Abby tilts her head and lets out a sigh. "If only you would have listened to me, Colton."

I ignore her and look at Mom, pointing to the phone. "What are you guys watching?"

Mom steps forward, using her soft voice, the breaking-bad-news voice. "Honey, I think you should..."

I snatch my phone from Abby. Again, I don't have time for Mom's pity or my sister's advice—advice I'm getting in heaps as I see the video titled, *Epic Fairy Fail*. And there's me on stage, frozen in failure, wearing tights and holding a wand, no less.

The tights, the wand, it's part of this New Faces theater thing at school—a trick to round up suckers and put them onstage to make fools of themselves. Mission accomplished. This year's title is *Gypsies and Fairies*, only there's just one fairy. Me.

Abby sits up straight and sets her arms out. "What were you doing, anyway? Walking like that on the stage. I mean, what is that?"

"I was flitting. Fairies flit."

Her hand doesn't make it to her mouth in time to stop the giggles.

"Abby," Mom coos. Her way of scolding my sister. Abby shrugs.

"Well, I could've helped, you know."

She gets back to arranging her playing cards spread out in front of her. Cards she thinks could have "protected me" from falling off the stage last night at rehearsals.

Abby is convinced I'm *cursed*. I remind her I'm on the football team. She reminds me I'm third string and never really play. "Still, I'm on the team."

"Yeah. Nice jersey."

It never ends around here. I go for the Captain Crunch and pour half of it on the counter because it's hard to roll your eyes and pour cereal at the same time. I sweep the scatter of cereal into my bowl, dump in the milk, snatch my phone, and lumber towards the table. Abby won't hear it. She stacks the twos and threes and so on in neat piles.

"When are you going to admit it?"

"When you admit you're not a witch."

She holds up a Jack of hearts. "For protection. Put it in your back pocket."

The last thing I need is help from my precocious little sister. It's bad enough she's skipped fifth grade and is only a single grade behind me now, it's even worse that because she gets straight A's, her antics are tolerated. Because I get straight C's, my life is under a microscope. Especially after play rehearsal last night.

I wipe back my hair and find a Captain Crunch stuck to my hand. "Please don't start with the Jacks. It's entirely too early for this."

"Suit yourself," she says with a giggle.

I shovel in three bites. Abby's smile reaches for her ears. I drop my spoon into the bowl. *Clank.* "What?"

She holds up the cards. "Get it? *Suit* yourself?"

Mom rubs her eyes and turns for the coffee maker. I get back to my phone. "I need to make sure that video didn't—" My phone buzzes. A text from Zach.

Dude ur famous.

Another buzz. This time a YouTube link. The same one my mother and sister were watching. This is not good.

Mom glances over her shoulder. "So how is your backside, sweetie?"

Abby snorts. I'm tempted to scatter her neat little piles of cards. She likes to arrange the spell casters and the spell protectors or—jeez, I'm embarrassed I even know what she's doing. I shake my head, refusing to play this game. "I'm fine, thanks for your concern."

Wiping the milk from my chin, I take a breath, then click on the link. My screen is cracked and splotchy—long story—but after a quick insurance ad, I'm staring at the plush red curtains of the Peakland High auditorium where we rehearse.

Action! And there's me, blissful, ignorant, digital me, about to take a fall at play rehearsal last night. Watching it now it's even worse than I thought. A bumbling fairy, helpless to the fate that lay before him. Attracted to a fall like iron to a magnet.

Mom eases up behind me, her feet crunching on the trail of cereal I've left behind. "How many views does it have now?" she asks.

I can practically hear Mom and Abby grinning. One head over each shoulder. Sometimes I think they speak to each other through some kind of female telepathy. I turn around, and their eyes widen in unison.

"Twenty-two-hundred hits," Abby announces. Mom shushes her just in time for my grand performance. There I go with my wand, teetering and wobbling before the slip, flip, and tumble into a podium, plummeting off the stage, sending a ladder crashing into the xylophone.

Lots of giggling. In the video and at the table.

"Such a shame," Abby says in her Mom voice. "Theater is no place for a clumsy fairy."

This time Mom doesn't even try to hide her laugh. But she cuts it short and points to the screen. "Is that Lani Andrews?"

Abby scoffs. "Why else would he be in the play, as a fairy no less?"

This is too much. I pocket my phone, check the clock on the microwave. "Well, gotta go."

"Such a sweet girl. I always liked her," Mom says.

"Yeah. Colton *likes* her, too."

I get to my feet and glare at my sister. Mom gives my shoulder a squeeze. "Oh sweetie, don't worry, it was just an accident. It happens to your father all the time."

"Oh my gosh," Abby gushes. "Remember when Dad fell off the ladder hanging the Christmas lights?"

"Or when he got tangled up in the mini-blinds," Mom adds, and they're off, reliving every mishap, pointing and giggling. I ignore them and get back to my phone, 2,268 now. I scroll to the comment section. (Tip: if you ever find yourself on YouTube, do not read the comments. Some things are better not seen.) Mom and Abby continue to live it up.

"What about when he hit himself in the head with the golf club?" Mom says, abandoning any hint of neutrality. From there they go on about the day Dad came home with that big hulking lump on his head. He'd been golfing with some guys at work, and well, the details are sketchy.

"The Clutts family curse," Abby says like a wise old crone. "I'm sure glad I'm protected. Aren't you, Mom?"

Mom sips her coffee and nods, lending legitimacy to Abby's foolishness. But I can't help myself. "So what about Dad?" I ask my sister, crossing my arms to hide the spread of chill bumps. "Why can't you 'protect' him?"

Abby holds up four jacks, tilting her head at me like I'm dense. "I'm afraid it's too late for Dad. He's too old and his curse is too strong." She leans in closer, getting all super dramatic. "But there's still hope for you. Maybe."

I scoff, but it's like I can't find my breath. Did I mention I hate curse talk? All the slips and scrapes over the years. Too many to count. Dad busting through the ceiling from the attic. His blackened fingernails whenever he uses a hammer, how he sometimes falls *up* the stairs. He spills and splatters, nicks and dents. Dad can crack fine china from three rooms away. And I'm his only son. Where Abby got the brains in the family, I inherited my father's dicey relationship with gravity.

"Colton," Mom says, breaking my trance, "just remember, the best thing we can do is to take caution. Slow down. That's what I tell your father. It's what Grandma told Papa. And what Great Grandma—"

"Mom, I got it."

"He's got it all right," Abby says, staring at my phone. She swipes and replays the video, and yep, this time I distinctly hear bells. And howls of laughter. Abby clicks her teeth. "He's got it bad."

I pat down my pockets. "How did you—" I snatch my phone from her again.

Being reminded that you've been hit with a family curse is not the best way to start your day, but neither is finding your stage tumble on YouTube. Anyway, I refuse to let some stupid superstition keep me down. I start for the sink but trip over the chair and the milk in my cereal bowl drenches my face. Abby and Mom gawk at me.

"Oh come on, that could happen to anyone," I say, blowing milk bubbles with "happen." I wipe my face with my shirt.

"Uh huh." Abby fans the deck of cards.

I stomp off for the bathroom, away from the snorting and giggling in the kitchen. A couple thousand views, that's not a whole lot, maybe no one at school saw it. Who am I kidding? I'm so dead.

I wash my face, work on my scowl again. Another half tuck of my jersey and I'm good to go. I toss a quick wave to Mom as I charge out the door.

Outside, a beautiful day is taking shape. I fiddle with the straps of my book bag and take in the fresh air. Sometimes I wait for Abby, but after all the laughing, the little thief can take her broom to school for all I care.

The leaves scrape along the street with my steps, a cool breeze finds my neck. I cut through a couple of yards, get grass on my shoes, and come out one street over, at Zach's house.

For the millionth time I tell myself it can't be that bad. And that's when I check my back pocket, where, just like yesterday, I find the four jacks. Maybe I should be more thankful Abby goes to all the trouble. Instead, just like yesterday, I toss them in Zach's trash can.

The door opens and Zach steps outside. He's about to start in on the video when he stops, looks at me, then to the trash can, and shakes his shaggy blond hair from his eyes.

"How does she do that, anyway?"

"I have no idea."

Acknowledgments

I usually end up with several versions of a novel. Not drafts, but completely different endings or subplots. But somewhere in the closing chapters of the final version of Fairy Dust Fumble, it became clear Abby was getting her own book. Still, I set it aside and worked on other projects. Then, during the long days of quarantine, as Fairy Dust Fumble was released to the world, I figured I'd give it a go. I wrote the first chapter, and just like Abby with those spells, there was no turning back.

As always, thanks to the entire Immortal Works Team. Staci for taking me in. To Holli, I really made you earn it this time! To Jason, Ruth, Katrina, and Lenore for the amazing cover designs. Thanks for everything. You guys are amazing.

Many thanks to Diane Fanning, for always being ready to talk. To Dad, for passing along the family curse. To Liz, the real life Abby. While she's moved on to new endeavors in the martial arts field, she got her start when I deemed her black belt worthy based on what I'd learned from the Karate Kid movies.

To James, who encouraged me to go on with Fairy Dust Fumble long after I'd given up on it. To Mom for all the support. To all the online support. It means a lot.

Lastly, to the fam. Simon, for reminding me how to be a kid. To Bella, for charming me every chance she gets. To my wife, Anne, who cleans up my messes and forces me outside my comfort zone when it comes to getting out the word about my books. Thanks for being the salesperson in the family.

About the Author

Pete Fanning is the author of several middle grade and young adult novels, including *Bricktown Boys*, winner of the 2021 Indies Today Best Juvenile Book award. He can be found at www.petefanning.com, where he's posted over 200 flash fiction stories.

This has been an
Immortal Production

Lightning Source UK Ltd.
Milton Keynes UK
UKHW010703101022
410232UK00004B/450